FRIEND OR FOE?

"You lookin' for him, mister?" asked the barkeep.

"Who?" Slocum knew who the bartender meant. Billy Quince was all anyone in El Paso talked about. The town was afire with the idea of a hanging.

"You got the look of a gunfighter. Killin' Quince is gonna increase any man's prestige."

"Any gunman's prestige," Slocum corrected. "I'm not a gunfighter."

"Yeah, sure," the barkeep said sarcastically.

Slocum had seen what the barkeep meant, though. Hard men with quick hands had moved into El Paso, waiting for a chance at Billy Quince.

Slocum let the tequila slip down his gullet. He drank to quench his thirst—and to let the alcohol remove what traces of duty he felt he owed Quince.

JAKE LOGAN

SLOCUM AND THE DEAD MAN'S SPURS

JOVE BOOKS, NEW YORK

SLOCUM AND THE DEAD MAN'S SPURS

A Jove Book / published by arrangement with
the author

PRINTING HISTORY
Jove edition / October 1999

The Penguin Putnam Inc. World Wide Web site address is
http://www.penguinputnam.com

ISBN: 0-515-12613-6

A JOVE BOOK®
Jove Books are published by The Berkley Publishing Group,
a division of Penguin Putnam Inc.,
375 Hudson Street, New York, New York 10014.
JOVE and the "J" design
are trademarks belonging to Penguin Putnam Inc.

PRINTED IN THE UNITED STATES OF AMERICA

10 9 8 7 6 5 4 3 2 1

SLOCUM AND THE
DEAD MAN'S SPURS

1

"Stampede!"

Slocum shot bolt upright when he heard the faint, echoing alarm from his partner, Billy Quince. He kicked free of his bedroll and jerked on his boots. Everything in the herders' camp around him moved now, stirring to an uneasy, disturbed life. The other cowhands working the Lazy V herd reacted slower than Slocum did. In the distance, from down in the valley, more of a vibration felt through the ground than actual sound, he heard—felt—the truth of Quince's warning.

Leaving his belongings behind, not even bothering to strap on his Colt in its cross-draw holster, he sprinted to the crude corral and found the dun-colored horse he had ridden for almost three months. The horse reacted to the unusual activity in the camp more than to the threat of possible death coming at them.

Or worse, Slocum knew, death voluntarily sought out by its rider. They had to stop the herd before it got to full speed. Otherwise, valuable beeves would die and Old Man Lacey would have a conniption fit over losing precious livestock. The Lazy V Ranch teetered on the brink of bankruptcy during the best of years, and this one wasn't all that good because of drought and sparse grama grass for the cattle to graze on, even in the higher elevations.

"Where you goin', Slocum?" demanded the top hand. Smitty—Slocum had never heard him called anything else—came sauntering up, more asleep than awake.

"Quince is out on night watch," Slocum said brusquely. "Stampede. I heard him plain as day."

Smitty scratched himself and shook his shaggy head.

"You're gettin' mighty worked up o'er nuthin'. None of the others heard a thing."

"The ground. Feel the rumble? It's not an earthquake." Slocum finished saddling his horse and swung its face around as he jumped into the saddle. The horse launched as though a rocket had been lit. The cold New Mexico desert air gusted past Slocum's face as he bent low and let the horse gallop. He couldn't keep up this flat-out pace long, but he wouldn't have to. It was only fifty yards to the rise where he could look down into the valley in the Sacramento Mountains where they had let the herd graze and water. He hoped Smitty was right, that he had confused a bad dream with the real thing.

Slocum didn't think so.

The alarm, the vibration in the ground, his gut feeling something was wrong—all hit the bull's-eye. He reined back and let his horse catch its breath as he tried to figure out what to do. The herd had shifted from where he had left it in Billy's capable hands. Slocum hated being an outrider for a herd, especially at night. It was lonely, dusty work and more tiring than roping and branding and birthing and the rest of the chores that needed doing for a herd this size.

He saw the massive dark lump spread over the ground ripple and rise up like some unholy outline on a blanket with a weasel trapped under it. The beeves looked to be running north, away from the pass. That let the cowboys down in their camp have another few minutes of living— until they got up here to try to turn the herd.

"Billy!" Slocum shouted. "Where are you?" The

pounding of cattle hooves drowned out his cries. Slocum tried to judge where his partner was most likely to ride. To one side of the black, undulating mass seemed the best bet. Billy would flank the herd, then try to find the leader and shoo him in the direction of the distant rocky escarpment rising up like a natural fence from the canyon floor.

Slocum got his reluctant horse moving again, heading for the side of the herd. Billy had good instincts and was a man Slocum had come to trust, walking up or going away.

A few of the frightened cattle charged at him as he made his way around the back edge of the herd. He avoided them, then turned and flanked the main body of frightened cows.

"Billy!"

"Here, Slocum, over here!" came the faint words. "Need help getting these damn steaks on the hoof to stop runnin'!"

Slocum galloped to his partner's side. Billy had a wild look about him and had lost his hat. Slocum doubted the younger cowboy had ever seen danger this close up before.

"You're doing good," Slocum said. "There, see the canyon face? Head 'em toward that."

"They'll kill themselves," Billy protested. "We'll have one hell of a mountain of steaks for chuck if they don't stop runnin' when they get to the cliff face."

"Let's ride!"

Side by side Slocum and Quince galloped, working their way in front of the frightened herd until they found the few cattle leading the stampede. Using his lariat, Slocum repeatedly whipped one steer's flanks until he broke it free of its fear and caused a flash of anger at the pummeling. The steer lowered its polled head and headed for Slocum to end the punishment he meted out so generously. Billy Quince worked at another cow and got it turned too.

Splitting the leaders and forcing them in different directions worked. Before the herd crashed into solid rock, the stampede dwindled, then faded into nothingness. A lot of exhausted cows milled around, wondering what had gone on. Grass that hadn't been cut up by pounding hooves provided solace, and within minutes the evidence of any danger had passed.

"I do declare, John, this one spooked me," Billy Quince admitted. He wiped his sweaty face with his bandanna. Looking around for his hat proved futile, and he gave up hoping to retrieve it. More than likely, it had been trampled to shreds under the herd's pounding hooves.

"What caused the stampede?" Slocum asked.

"I got some suspicions, but I can't rightly say for sure."

Before Billy could say any more, Smitty and a half-dozen cowhands rode up.

"You done good, you two. Sorry I didn't pick up on the warning, Slocum. Reckon I don't wake up too good without a cup of coffee sloshin' in my belly."

"No real harm done," Slocum said, glancing at Billy.

Billy Quince cleared his throat and said, "Somebody spooked the herd. On purpose."

"Why'd anyone do a damnfool thing like that?" asked Smitty.

"Rustlers," Billy said. "I can't be sure, but think I heard the crack of a bullwhip. A few well-placed whacks on the backside of a steer and, well, a stampede is about what you'd expect."

"Cain't count the beeves, not till morning," said Smitty, looking glum. "Even then, we'd have to round up strays to be sure we're missin' any."

"How certain are you about rustlers causing the stampede?" Slocum asked Billy.

"Real sure, John."

That was all Slocum needed. He trusted Billy's judgment.

"You ain't sayin' that' to cover up yer own incompetence, now are you?" asked a runty little troublemaker named Guynes. "You fall asleep out here and the herd gets spooked at a rattler or something and you got a stampede you might have prevented."

"The only rattler out here is riding a chestnut mare," Billy said, staring Guynes down.

"Why, you—" Guynes made for his hogleg. Smitty reached out and batted the man's hand away from the butt of his six-shooter.

"Don't go gettin' riled, you two," Smitty said. "Nobody's sayin' you done anythin' but yer best, Quince. And you, Guynes, shut that pie hole of yours."

Guynes glowered, jerked at his reins, and took off. Smitty shrugged and made his way through the center of the herd to be sure the cattle were settling down.

"Rustlers," Billy said firmly.

Slocum nodded, then joined Smitty to be sure danger of another stampede was far, far off.

"Danged near a hundred head gone," grumbled Slim Lacey. The old man's wrinkled face curled up like a prune as he spat into the fire. A wispy column of steam rose, not a hint of wind causing it to drift. Slocum watched in rapt fascination, more interested in insignificant things like smoke than what the rancher said. He had heard it all from the owners of other herds. Never enough grass or water, Texas fever, something.

"So, boys, what do you think?"

"I think there wasn't enough carcasses to make up for a hundred lost cows," said Billy Quince. "I found a couple what was sufferin'. Shot 'em to put them out of their misery, but that was all. Wasn't more than ten of them."

"We cooked 'em, Boss. Just like always," said Smitty.

"So we lost a hundred head to rustlers. No other explanation," Lacey said. "I can't stand to lose more."

"What are you saying?" asked Slocum.

"I'm offering you and Billy the chance to run them varmints to ground. You're makin' fifteen dollars a month and vittles now. I'll give you a hundred dollars to track them down."

"That much?" asked Billy, his eyes going wide. It might

be more money than he'd ever seen in one lump.

"Each," Slim Lacey declared.

"Why us?" asked Slocum, but he knew the reason. Most of the other cowboys had worked for Lacey several seasons. Some were old-timers, others hardly wet behind the ears. Only he and Billy had the look of men capable of tracking—and killing. Slocum rested his hand on the worn ebony butt of his Colt Navy. He had seen death in his day, maybe too much.

He had protested Quantrill's raid on Lawrence, Kansas, and had been gutshot for not wanting to murder eight-year-old boys. By the time he had healed and returned to Slocum's Stand in Calhoun County, Georgia, his parents were dead. His brother, Robert, had died during Pickett's Charge. Hardly knowing he did it, Slocum reached and fingered the watch in his vest pocket—his only legacy from his brother.

But the life of a gentlemen farmer wasn't meant to be his. A carpetbagger judge had taken a fancy to the spread and worked hard on papers showing no taxes had been paid on the land throughout the war. The crooked judge and his hired gun had ridden out one fine day to take Slocum's Stand from its rightful owner.

They had succeeded far beyond their dreams. They remained on the land—six feet under near the springhouse. Slocum had ridden West, and had dodged wanted posters offering a reward for judge-killing.

That hadn't been his only crime, but it was the one that never seemed to be forgotten.

"I can use this," he said. "A hundred dollars is a powerful lot of money unless you want us to gun the rustlers down."

"I want them stopped. Run 'em off, gun 'em down, get the worthless sheriff to arrest them, I don't give a good goddamn," Lacey said hotly. "I can't afford to lose more beeves."

"We'll do it," Billy said quickly, glancing sideways at Slocum, worried his partner might decline such a magnanimous offer. Slocum shrugged. He didn't mind riding herd. It was grueling work, but honest work. It just didn't pay well. With the kind of reward Slim Lacey offered, he and Billy could move on sooner rather than later.

All they'd have to do was figure out where the rustlers had headed—and not get killed by them.

"Then get to it!" Lacey cried. "The sooner you find those sidewinders' burrow and stopper it up, the sooner you'll get your money."

Slocum and Quince rode from camp in silence, but Slocum saw his partner was boiling over.

"I thought you was goin' to tell him to stuff it, John. One hundred dollars! That's a fortune!"

"Had more," Slocum said laconically.

"But I *need* it," Billy said. "That telegram I got 'fore we came out with the herd? My sister, Lizbeth, is all alone now. My folks died from cholera, and I want to bring her on out here so she can be with me." Billy eyed Slocum and grinned almost shyly. "I reckon you and Lizbeth might hit it off."

"You wouldn't want me as a brother-in-law," Slocum said.

"Hell and damnation, John, I wouldn't mind if you was my *brother*. There's nothin' I wouldn't do for you."

"Then get to tracking," Slocum said. They neared the area where the herd had grazed the night before. Stampedes tore up the ground, but something might have been left by the rustlers to show where they'd headed with their hundred head of stolen cattle.

"Lookee here, John," Billy said, dropping to one knee. "Looks like a powerful lot of cattle came this way—away from the direction of the stampede."

Slocum had also dismounted. He held up a six-inch piece of worn leather he had found caught on a thorn bush.

"That looks the world like the cracker off a whip," Billy said.

"Just the thing to get cattle moving—or stampeding."

Together they followed the trail until it was obvious a small herd of cattle had been driven up and over a pass leading to the north. Slocum took a deep breath, sampled some of the water he had in a canteen, and then said, "We may be up against it, Billy. You know who we're trailing?"

"Paddy Patterson, 'less I miss my guess," Quince said. "If we have to go up against a rustler, might as well go 'gainst the king of 'em all."

Slocum sat on a rock and stared into the hills, wondering if he hadn't bitten off more than he could chew. The law had tried to bring Paddy Patterson in for years and had always failed. Of late, the outlaw had become bolder, taking risks no sane man would choose. Besides rustling, Patterson was hunted for train robbing and then holding up a bank down in El Paso not a week later. Even the Apaches had taken to giving him a wide berth.

Crazy Gun, they called him now.

"A hundred dollars doesn't seem enough anymore," Slocum said.

"I need the money, John. Truly. I can't let Lizbeth rot. She's my little sister."

Slocum heaved to his feet. "Might be we can track Patterson down and then let the law know where his hideout is. We could get a few dollars reward money without getting our hides ventilated."

Billy Quince nodded curtly and mounted. They set off into the mountain fastness where the rustlers ruled. Slocum wasn't sure how far they had to go before finding the outlaws. Somehow, he wasn't surprised when he spotted a sentry high in the rocks less than a mile up the trail.

Slocum tugged at Billy's sleeve and pointed. They got their horses off the trail and dismounted.

"He never saw us," Quince said breathlessly. "What do we do now? Take him out?"

"That might be worse than letting him finish his cigarette," Slocum said. "I'll scout ahead and—"

"No!" Billy took a deep breath. "I'm not lettin' you do

all the work. We're partners and in this together.''

Slocum shrugged, then motioned for Billy to come along. They made their way through the tumble of rocks beneath the sentry's post. The man smoked the cigarette that had taken his attention off the trail. The smell of tobacco smoke wafting down made Slocum suck in a deep breath. After they scouted Paddy Patterson's hideout he would fix himself a smoke too. He would have earned it.

The two drifted through the rock and followed a canyon wall until a different type of smoke reached Slocum's twitching nose.

"Pinyon," he said. "Cooking fire." Slocum moved on and then fell flat on his belly. Beside him Billy went to ground also. Not ten feet in front of them strutted a man. All Slocum could see were flashing silver spurs with Spanish rowels clanking behind the heels of scuffed boots.

"Paddy Patterson," whispered Quince. "I heard tell he wore fancy spurs."

Slocum rose like a lizard and craned his neck to get a better look at the camp. To his surprise, he saw only two other rustlers in addition to Patterson. And of the cattle he saw, heard, and smelled nothing.

"The gang must be getting the beeves to a railroad for shipment, or they have them somewhere else," Slocum said.

"Would Lacey need for us to find the cattle 'fore he pays up?"

Slocum only wanted to get the hell away from the rustlers' camp. He had started creeping back when something gave him away. It might have been something Billy did. More likely, Slocum had crossed Lady Luck.

"Intruders!" shouted Paddy Patterson. The man slapped leather and drew out a huge Smith & Wesson. The report echoed through the canyon as the slug missed Slocum's head by inches.

Rolling to his left, Slocum stopped, then rolled right, getting his own six-shooter out. The Colt Navy was only

.36-caliber, but he was a better shot than the rustler. Slocum caught Patterson in the side, spinning the man around.

"Let's hightail it," he called to Billy. But the other men were already on their feet, six-shooters out and blazing away. Quince caught one of the other two outlaws in the middle of the forehead. The man fell backward into the campfire. His shirt catching fire distracted his partner long enough for Slocum to get to his feet, take careful aim, and fire. Slocum's slug ripped through the man's chest. His second round killed the rustler outright.

"Die, you son of a bitch!" came the angry curse. From the corner of his eye Slocum saw Paddy Patterson lifting his heavy six-gun. All Slocum could focus on was the huge bore and how he looked smack down it. It was big enough to crawl into.

Slocum had been in tight spots before. Now he knew he was going to die.

He flinched when the sharp crack sounded like a death knell in his ears. But the pain and darkness of death never followed. Slocum swung toward Patterson, going into a crouch. He was ready to put an end to the rustler's foul life.

Billy Quince had beaten him to it. Quince stood with his six-shooter smoking and his hand shaking just a little. He stared at the fallen outlaw.

"Never killed a man before," Quince said, a catch in his voice. He was pale under his weather-beaten tan and his hand shook.

"You haven't yet," Slocum said, going to the fallen rustler's side. Eyes filled with madness and hate glared up at Slocum. He kicked Patterson's six-shooter away from his feebly twitching fingers.

"You think you done kilt me," Paddy Patterson said in a surprisingly strong voice. "You done me a big favor."

"The only favor we've done anyone," said Billy Quince, "was for the ranchers you've been rustling from." A measure of bravado had returned to the young man now that the shooting was over.

"You win," Patterson said, sneering. "Go on. Take my spurs. You deserve 'em."

Billy looked at Slocum.

"To the victor belongs the spoils," Slocum said. He didn't cotton much to robbing a dead man, but Paddy Patterson was still alive, if not kicking too much. And he had offered them to Quince. That struck Slocum as odd since Paddy Patterson wasn't known as a charitable man.

Billy pounced on them like a cougar on a wounded deer. He pulled off the outlaw's spurs and sat in the dirt as he put them on his own boots. The silver wheels caught the sunlight in a crazy rainbow as he spun the rowels.

"These surely do look mighty fine," he said to Patterson, standing so he could look at his newly won Mexican silver spurs. "And we're getting a hefty reward for you and your worthless gang."

"Burn in Hell, you stupid bastard! Those spurs are cursed!" Paddy Patterson laughed harshly, then coughed up blood. He stared straight at Billy Quince but without a hint of malice. Slocum had never seen anything like it. If he hadn't known better, he would have thought the rustler was glad to die.

2

"I can't believe this, John, I truly cannot," Billy Quince said happily, leafing through the wad of greenbacks he had received from the sheriff in Tularosa. "With the reward from Lacey throwed in, my share is danged near three hundred dollars. I've never had this much money at one time in my whole danged life."

Slocum felt a similar wad of bills in his own shirt pocket. Unlike his partner, he didn't flash the money in public. Tularosa was a wide-open town, but he had to admit they were given wide berth by the citizens. They had brought down Paddy Patterson and his gang of rustlers. That made them powerful hombres to be avoided.

"Who'd've thought a man like Patterson carried such a big reward on his head?" Slocum said. They headed for the ramshackle Rosebud Saloon. When they entered, the din inside dropped to a whisper, then picked up again when they moved to the far end of the bar without bothering anyone. Slocum didn't like the way every eye followed them like a cat following a mouse—or worse, like a mouse worried about a nearby tomcat's hunger. He had made a practice of staying in the shadows. It was only chance that his face hadn't shown up on a wanted poster in the stack on the sheriff's desk.

13

"Howdy, gents. Here you go," said the small, wiry barkeep as he shoved a bottle of whiskey toward them. "It's on the house."

"That's mighty friendly of you," Quince said.

"Why?" asked Slocum, suspicious of anything for free. He had been in too many gin mills where a free drink carried a dose of chloral hydrate along with it. Get the victim a bit dizzy, slug him, and rob him. That was the only way some saloons kept in business.

"You're notorious, the two of you," the barkeep replied. "You're good advertisin' for the Rosebud, if you keep drinkin' here and don't shoot nobody. 'Less they deserve it, of course," the barkeep added hastily, as if he might have offended their sensibilities.

"You mean folks would come on by to have a look at us?" Quince shook his head in amazement. "Never been famous before. I think I could get to likin' it. How about you, Slocum?"

Slocum wanted to leave, but if he did the men in the saloon would gossip. No fuss, that was the way he lived his life. He took a drink and held it up to the barkeep.

"To luck," he said.

This seemed to please everyone, including Billy Quince. Quince knocked back a drink and hastily poured another, as if the desert heat would suck the bottle dry if he didn't finish it first.

"Never seen you drink like this," Slocum said.

"Never saw me when I had anything to celebrate."

"You send for your sister yet?" Slocum asked.

"Just on my way to the Western Union station to wire her the money. Reckon El Paso is as close to civilization as she can get on the stage."

"As I remember it, the Butterfield line runs to the east of town," Slocum said. "There's a depot at Hueco Tanks ten miles outside of El Paso."

"Then I'll have Lizbeth go to El Paso. We can decide

from there where to go. Maybe San Francisco. She might like living high on the hog there.''

''You don't have the money for that,'' Slocum said.

''No, but the way I look at it, Paddy Patterson was easy. There are outlaws all over the place. Bring in a few and get rich.''

''Bounty hunters don't enjoy long lives. Word gets out and men shoot them in the back, even men who aren't being hunted.''

''Slocum, you're about the sorriest excuse for a man I ever saw,'' Quince said hotly. ''Cheer up. Drink. Get loose and enjoy yourself. I'm a hero and want to relish the feel.''

''We didn't do anything heroic,'' Slocum said. ''All we did was work mighty hard at staying alive.''

''Might be what you did, but *I* was a damned hero!'' Quince shouted. Heads turned and a deathly silence fell in the saloon. ''You take back callin' me a coward.''

''Never said that,'' Slocum said. ''You saved my hide back there, and I owe you for that.''

''That's better. I accept your apology,'' Quince said loudly. ''But next time, you don't have to crawl like a whipped dog when you offer up an apology.''

Slocum went cold inside. He didn't take that from any man, even one he had come to call partner.

''Relax, John, relax. It was just a joke,'' Quince said. ''I'm just feelin' my oats.'' He swallowed another mouthful of the potent liquor. ''Need to get the telegraph station and wire my sister some money. You keep my place, and I'll be back 'fore you know it.''

Slocum watched Quince swagger from the saloon. His newly won silver spurs jangled musically as he walked. As Quince stepped into the sun-washed street, a brilliant ray of light reflected from the spurs, momentarily blinding Slocum. When his vision came back, Quince had vanished as if he had turned to smoke and blown away on the hot desert wind.

''Hope you don't mind me sayin' this,'' said the barkeep,

"but your partner's headed for some big trouble if he don't shut his yap. There's some folks in Tularosa what don't take kindly to a man spoutin' off like that."

"You're right," Slocum said. "I'm one of them."

He worked on his drink and considered what they were going to do next. Slim Lacey, his herd, and the Lazy V were miles away over in the Sacramento Mountains. He and Quince had come to Tularosa with the outlaws' bodies to claim their reward. With the bounty money burning a hole in his pocket, Slocum wasn't inclined to go back to punching cattle. And he sure as hell and damnation wasn't going to turn bounty hunter. He hated them as much as he did lice gnawing at his flesh.

Billy had hinted more than once how he thought Slocum and his sister Lizbeth would hit it off. Slocum decided to ride on down to El Paso with Quince and see his sister safely off the stage. After that, he would play it by ear. Billy's braggadocio wasn't the way Slocum liked a partner to behave. There was nothing but trouble on the horizon if he didn't quiet down.

Still, he had the right to brag a little. This was the first time Billy had done anything anyone else considered worthwhile. Paddy Patterson had turned into a hellish tornado whirling through the entire Tularosa Basin, killing and stealing and raping as he went. No one was likely to shed a tear over his passing.

"How long you and your partner stayin' around town?" asked the barkeep.

"Not long," said Slocum. On impulse he asked, "How long had Patterson been hurrahing the area?"

"Paddy? He was born not far from here, up in Carrizozo. Spent his life doin' some rustling mostly, leastwise until about three months back. Then he really cut loose."

"That when he started killing?"

"Anything that moved," the barkeep agreed. "Didn't make no never mind to him if it was man, women, child, or rattler.'' The barkeep shook his head sadly. ''Never saw a man go that bad that fast.''

Slocum said nothing. Quince came back into the saloon, standing in the doorway until he was sure everyone saw his dramatic entrance.

''Them spurs he's wearin','' said the barkeep. ''Those were Paddy's, weren't they?'' Before Slocum could answer, Billy kicked up a ruckus.

''You need a good bath. You smell like a pile behind my horse,'' Billy said, singling out a tall, bulky man wearing a serape slung over his shoulder. Slocum didn't make the man to be Mexican, but under his dark tan it was hard to tell.

''What you saying?'' the man asked, standing and kicking back the chair. From under the serape Slocum saw the man had a sawed-off shotgun slung on a leather strap. If trouble developed, Billy Quince would be cut in half before he could get his six-shooter halfway out of his holster.

''You're a stinking Mexican, that's what I'm sayin','' Quince said, squaring off.

Slocum moved fast, walking between the men. His arms caught Billy's and held them firmly to his side. He grunted as he picked Quince up and carried him through the door. Over his shoulder, Slocum said, ''Too much tarantula juice. The rest of our bottle's all yours, amigo.''

''What are you doin', John? Didn't you hear how that stinkin', good-for-nothing Mexican insulted me?''

''I didn't hear anything of the sort,'' Slocum said outside. ''Did you wire your sister the money?''

''She needs more than I had,'' Billy said, his mood changing mercurially when Slocum mentioned Lizbeth. ''Another hundred and I can get her to El Paso, but—''

''Here, take this,'' Slocum said, handing Billy the money from his own poke.

''John, I can't—''

''Do it. I got some debts to pay around town from last time I rode through here. The stable owner's going to be surprised and mighty happy when I pay him. Now get on out of here, and I'll see you later. Stay out of trouble.''

The laugh sounded more like the old Billy Quince he remembered. But a hint of derision rode with the once-joyful sound as Billy strutted back to the telegraph station with Slocum's money clutched in his hand. Slocum shook his head, then went to pay his old bills.

Not surprisingly, it took most of the money he had remaining, but he was content. He didn't owe anyone in Tularosa a dime. That was the way a man ought to live, owning no one anything.

Slocum lost the last of his stake to the gambler across the table from him. He eyed the man. The tinhorn had probably been cheating, but he had done it so well Slocum couldn't figure out how it was done. If nothing else, the man deserved his money for being so clever—or dexterous with hideout cards.

''That does me in, gents,'' Slocum said, pushing back from the table.

''I'll spot you a few dollars,'' offered the gambler, but Slocum knew better than to accept. He would end up in debt again, and there was no telling what the gambler might want him to do to clear the obligation. Men like this had markers scattered all over the territory. Slocum wasn't inclined to become the gambler's collector of bad debts.

''Thanks, maybe later,'' Slocum said, going to the bar. The barkeep gave him another free drink. This was about the only consolation Slocum had. He had given Billy a sizable portion of his money to get his sister to El Paso, then paid bills and lost the rest. He was stone broke, after being flush only that morning.

It didn't bother him too much. He could always go back to the Lazy V and punch cattle for the rest of the season.

''Yahoo!'' came the loud cry from the door. Slocum went into a crouch, his hand flashing for his Colt Navy when a gunshot sounded. He didn't draw when he saw Billy in the doorway, gun in hand.

The man swaggered to the bar and accepted the free drink as if it was his due. Quince turned and stared at the others in the room, then belligerently called out, "What's the matter? Never seen a hero before? Well, here I am!"

The barkeep looked imploringly at Slocum.

"You been doing some heavy drinking?" Slocum asked.

"No, why'd you say that? I been goin' around to see if the good people of Tularosa really appreciate what I done."

Slocum said nothing. Billy had conveniently forgotten there had been two of them in Paddy Patterson's camp.

"John," Billy said, sidling closer, "I need a few more dollars to tide me over."

"Just lost the last I had to that gambler," Slocum said, pointing with his chin Navajo style, indicating the man in the cutaway jacket.

"He musta cheated you. You're the best damned gambler I ever seen!"

Slocum put a hand on Billy's arm to restrain him. "I lost. Luck comes and goes. It just wasn't with me tonight. Let him be."

Billy jerked free and turned his back to the room. The way he was acting, Slocum wondered how much longer Billy Quince would be able to do that without worrying about some young buck emptying a six-gun into his back.

"John, I need money real bad." He cleared his throat and looked at Slocum. "I heard something that might do both of us a world of good."

"What's that?"

"A shipment of gold's comin' into town tonight. There's a way station outside of town where they change horses. That'd be about perfect for an ambush."

"You wanting me to help you rob a stagecoach?" Slocum wasn't sure he'd heard Billy Quince right. Quince had always been foursquare for upholding the law. The most unlawful thing Slocum had ever seen him do was spit on the boardwalk in Lincoln.

"Why not? The two of us can do it easy. I reckon there might be a thousand dollars worth of bullion on that stage."

Slocum considered the matter a spell. He wasn't above robbing a stagecoach now and then, but usually when he had no prospects at all.

"We can go back to herding for Lacey," he said. "We never told him we were quitting."

"That's for suckers, John. I want *big* money. You don't want to track down outlaws for the rewards on their heads, but you can't say anything against this. We can be down in El Paso with the gold 'fore they even know it's gone."

Slocum considered what his partner said. A quick robbery might give the chance for them to part company. Billy was starting to wear him down. The money had gone to Billy's head and turned him downright nasty, something Slocum had never seen in Quince before.

If Billy and his sister headed for San Francisco, it might be time for Slocum to see if any of the fancy riverboats still plied the muddy Mississippi River.

"A thousand dollars?" Slocum mused. "That's more than we made off Paddy Patterson."

"Exactly right," Billy said earnestly. "We can do it and be out of the territory 'fore they know anything happened. I know you've stuck up stagecoaches before, John. You never bragged on it, but I know you did. I feel it in my bones."

"Let's look over the situation," Slocum said. The whiskey had turned bitter on his tongue, and his boots itched to be moving in some other direction. Any direction away from Billy Quince.

After they lightened the stagecoach of a load of gold bullion.

They rode out of Tularosa and into the malpais. The land was ugly and as dangerous as any Slocum had ever seen. Even the Apaches treated this part of the territory with respect. Hot during the day, cold at night, deadly all the time.

They rode in silence, each wrapped in his own thoughts, until they topped a rise overlooking the way station.

"There she is, John. Just like I said."

"There's a stage changing horses. I thought we were just scouting the area and waiting for the bullion to come along later."

"No, sir, that's the shipment," Billy insisted. "We can stick up the stage as it rumbles along the road and heads for the bend."

"How do you know that? You ever been in this part of the country before?"

"I—I don't know," Billy said, momentarily confused. He recovered and his voice changed, dropping lower, sounding more confident, more belligerent. "You in or out? I can spend the money all by myself."

Slocum traced the stagecoach route from his vantage point and saw Billy was probably right. How did he know, though? They had ridden together for a spell and never come this way. Quince had never mentioned being here before they brought in the rustlers for the reward. As far as Slocum had ever heard, Billy Quince was a Kansas boy, born and bred. He hadn't left home until he was eighteen and he started wandering. To judge from his tall tales of the Dakotas, he had explored up north for a couple years before dropping down to Fort Griffin, where he and Slocum had teamed up.

But he had unerringly picked the best spot for a holdup.

"We do it now, John. No holdin' back." Billy pulled up his bandanna so it covered his face. Then he drew his six-shooter. He didn't wait to see if Slocum was following as he rode off, waving the six-gun in the air.

Slocum heaved a sigh, pulled up his bandanna, and then lit out after Quince. He had a bad feeling, but Billy was no man's fool. He owed Billy his life a couple times over and could trust him this one last time.

"Stand and deliver!" Quince yelled to the driver. The

shotgun messenger lifted his long-barreled weapon, then settled down when he saw Billy had the drop on him.

"Don't go gettin' antsy, young'n," the grizzled old driver said. "We ain't got nuthin' you want."

"You have a strongbox crammed full of bullion, you lyin' old fart!"

Slocum rode up in time to see the driver and guard exchanged puzzled looks. The driver shook his head.

"You got the wrong stage. Never carry gold. Hardly ever carry anything but mail into Tularosa. Yer welcome to that." He bent down to pull out the box when Billy shot him.

"What?" The shotgun messenger saw the driver slump forward and tumble from the box. He grabbed for his shotgun. Billy Quince put a slug through his heart before he could lift the gun.

"What are you doing?" demanded Slocum. "They did what you said and you shot them!"

"Get the passengers outside now," snapped Quince. "They must have something worth stealin'."

Two women and a man came from the coach, fearful of what would happen. They saw that both driver and guard had been shot dead. The man moved to protect the two women.

"That's all," Slocum said. "There's no bullion. Let's get out of here."

"No!" Billy swung his six-shooter around and pointed it at Slocum, his hand shaking in rage. Then he moved back to cover the male passenger. "I want your wallet and all your jewelry. You look like some fancy-ass gambler loaded down with gold and diamond stickpins."

"All I got is in here," the man said, reaching for his wallet in an inner coat pocket.

Billy Quince shot the man through the head. The women screamed and clung to each other for support.

"Why'd you go and do that?" Slocum was aghast at the cold-blooded murder.

"He was goin' for a hideout gun. I know it."

"He wasn't armed," one woman cried. "He was a good man, and you murdered him!"

"Billy!" snapped Slocum as Quince lifted his six-gun to shoot the woman. "Enough. There's nothing for us here."

"They cheated me. There was supposed to be gold."

Slocum climbed into the box and pulled out the strongbox. He shot off the lock and threw open the lid. Slocum looked up, his green eyes cold.

"There's only mail in here. No bullion, no coins, not even any greenbacks."

"They hid it. They did it to make me mad."

"You're a horrible man!" shouted the bolder—or dumber—of the women. Slocum saw how Billy Quince fought against killing the woman. Both women. And how he was slowly losing the battle. He had already murdered three men. What was a pair of women to him now that he had tasted blood and liked it?

"I'm getting out of here," Slocum said, distracting his former partner. Slocum could put up with outrageous behavior, but not murder for the sheer thrill of killing. What had changed Billy Quince he couldn't say, and it didn't much matter to him.

"Wait, we can get it out of them. They know. They have to know where the gold is!"

Slocum jumped from the top of the stage and rode away, expecting to hear two more shots to mark the end of more lives. He ought to have stopped Billy Quince, but he owed him.

Slocum winced as the shots rang out. He *had* owed Quince. The blood debt was paid. He put his heels to the horse's flanks and headed in the one direction he reckoned Billy Quince would never ride.

3

"Hey, Slocum, I got a newspaper from the ranch. It's only a week old."

Slocum looked up, wondering what had gotten Smitty so worked up over a newspaper. Now and then Slim Lacey sent out a copy of the *Las Vegas Optic,* as if anyone really cared about what the Santa Fe politicians did as seen by an army of reporters even farther north. More important was the chance of rain bringing some relief to the crushing heat. If the Lazy V herd didn't get new water soon, they would have to move the beeves into higher pastures. That was more important than anything he would read in a newspaper.

Smitty tossed the rolled-up paper to Slocum, who easily caught it. The well-read newspaper fell open to the front page. Slocum swallowed hard when he saw the headlines.

"That there's your ole partner, ain't it, Slocum?"

Slocum read down the column of print quickly. He finished, folded the paper, and handed it back to the top hand.

"He was," Slocum said. "He rode a different trail after we split in Tularosa."

"You drunk up your money. Billy Quince now, he's out there makin' a real name for hisself."

Slocum knew Smitty was trying to rile him. Ever since

the rustlers had been caught, the cowboys had looked up to Slocum for leadership and not to Smitty. This was the man's way of getting some measure of respect back—showing Slocum how his former partner had turned into a cold-blooded murderer.

The report showed a path of death and destruction seldom seen in even as rough a territory as New Mexico. Something had rotted inside Billy Quince to make him capable of such atrocities. Men shot in the back—and then he bragged about it. Robberies for a few dollars that left behind corpses. Quince had robbed a Soccoro bank of eighty dollars and had killed three tellers and a woman customer. It didn't matter to him who looked down the barrel of his deadly six-shooter. Man or woman, it didn't matter as long as they died by his hand.

What caught Slocum's attention most in the story was the report of a fight where Billy Quince had outdrawn a notorious gunman. Slocum had never seen any talent, any quickness, any gun-handling skill in the young man to credit the account. But the viciousness of firing until his six-gun was empty matched what Slocum had seen before parting company with Quince.

"Whatcha make of it, Slocum? Billy Quince turnin' into a backshootin' owlhoot?"

" 'Bout the same as you, I reckon," Slocum said, not wanting to bandy words with Smitty.

"Well, I think he ought to swing at the end of a rope."

"Can't argue," Slocum said, remembering the botched stagecoach robbery. He ought to have stopped Quince then and there, but his sense of obligation had slowed him. And deep down, he had not thought Billy would kill unarmed men and defenseless women.

"Maybe you ought to be hangin' alongside him when the law finally catches him."

"Don't like the way I rope and brand?" Slocum asked. This produced a chuckle from several cowboys listening hard to their trail boss and Slocum.

"You . . ." Smitty never got any farther. Slim Lacey came riding up with a tired-looking man sitting beside him in the buggy. The owner of the Lazy V worked hard to get a gimpy leg out of the buggy and under him before jumping to the ground. The man with him proved more agile. As he turned, the badge on his vest caught the sun and momentarily dazzled Slocum.

Slocum didn't have to be a traveling medicine show mind reader to know what had brought out the rancher and the federal marshal.

Billy Quince.

"Slocum, I want a word with you. This here's Marshal Hanssen, out of Santa Fe. He's come to track down your old partner."

"Marshal," Slocum said, eyeing the man. Dull eyes told of long days in the saddle before additional dust-eating in Lacey's buggy. Slow reflexes convinced Slocum he had nothing to fear. This was a man staggering along the edge of exhaustion, and he hadn't come to put up a fight.

Slocum always worried about the wanted posters carrying his likeness. To a man like Smitty, even a fifty-dollar reward would be a fortune, especially if it came from turning over an hombre he didn't like to the law.

"You rode with Quince, didn't you?" Hanssen asked.

"You know I did or you wouldn't be here. What can I do for you?" Slocum stared straight at Lacey.

"I was tellin' the marshal how you and Billy brought the Paddy Patterson gang to justice."

"Kilt the lot of them," said Smitty. "They murdered them, just like Billy's done to all them other gents."

"We shot it out with them," Slocum said. "There wasn't any hint we backshot a one of them."

"Ain't sayin' you did, Slocum," Hanssen said. "I been talkin' to Mr. Lacey, and he says you're about the only man likely to even find Billy Quince, much less bring him down."

"I won't shoot my former partner."

"Then track him down for us. He's movin' too fast for even a posse to follow. Find him and let me know how to arrest him. This killin's gettin' out of hand."

"How many's he killed?"

Marshal Hanssen sucked on his teeth a moment, then said, "Best we can tell, he's up to ten men now. Then there's the two Mexicans. And three women. There's no stoppin' him."

"I read about some of his exploits," Slocum said. "What you're telling me is that it's worse than reported?"

"That story don't hit the mark by a country mile. Quince has declared war on the entire New Mexico Territory. If I thought it'd do a whit of good, I'd have the cavalry out after him. But . . ." Marshal Hanssen shook his head sadly.

"What's wrong with that? The Ninth Cavalry has some mighty fine soldiers riding under its banner."

"That's part of the problem, Slocum. Quince made the boast he'll kill every Mexican and Negro he comes across. From what he's done so far, there's no reason to doubt him."

Slocum said nothing. The Ninth was a buffalo soldier unit. Billy Quince would have only to shoot in their general direction to hit a black man. Slocum frowned as he considered all the marshal had said. Never once while he had ridden with Quince had the man shown such strong feelings against Mexicans and black men. For all that, he had never shown the streak of mean that had turned him into a stone killer.

His killing ways had started when they had shot it out with the rustlers.

"Cursed spurs," grumbled Slocum.

"How's that?" asked the marshal.

"Nothing. I don't know if I can find him."

"Look, Slocum, there's a heap of money on his head, but I don't want you turnin' bounty hunter, not with your own partner," Lacey said. "What I want is for you to shoo him out of the territory."

"Now wait, Mr. Lacey. I—"

"Marshal," the rancher said sharply. "You can't stop him. Might be Slocum can chase him off."

"He ought to swing," Hanssen said. "Them's *federal* charges against him. Nothing less would bring me this far from Santa Fe."

"I'm not disputin' that, Marshal, but if you can't get a hemp necktie around his throat, isn't this the next best thing? Let someone else deal with him. Maybe the Texas Rangers. They got an over-inflated view of themselves."

"Where was Quince last seen?" Slocum asked.

"Over in Las Cruces. The man rides like the wind. One week he's in the north, the next he's south. He steals enough horses to ride till one drops, then switches to another. That's one reason we're in such a fine pickle trackin' him," Marshal Hanssen said.

"Two months' pay, Slocum," Lacey said. "That's what I'm offerin' if you run him off. Then you come on back, and I'll see about gettin' you a better job."

Smitty's eyes went wide at this. The only job better than cowhand was foreman—and that meant him.

"No need for that, Mr. Lacey," Slocum said. "I'll take the two months of pay and see what I can do. I've got an idea or two where he might be headed."

"Tell me and—"

"He wouldn't let you within a mile, Marshal," Slocum said. "Besides, this might just be a job for the Rangers, as Mr. Lacey said."

Lacey nodded curtly. He and the federal marshal climbed back into the buggy and rattled off. Slocum wasted no time getting his gear packed and hitting the trail for El Paso. That was about the only place Billy Quince might be heading—for El Paso and his sister.

Slocum let the tequila slip down his gullet and pool in his belly. He felt like he was going to puke. The tequila was strong, but the word of how Billy Quince had massacred an entire family out west of El Paso caused the real upset in Slocum's gut. There had been no question about the identity of the man who had robbed the Nance family, killing father, mother, and three children. He had spent the better part of a day carving his full name into the side of their wagon.

"If I got that son of a buck in my sights, I wouldn't bring him in," declared a drunk down the bar from Slocum. "I'd send him to the promised land, just like he has a dozen others."

"Promised land?" snorted the cowboy next to him. "To Hell, I'd say. There's no room in Heaven for a man like Billy Quince."

Slocum stared at the painting of the nude woman behind the bar, seeing nothing. He drank to quench his thirst—and to let the alcohol remove what traces of obligation he felt he owed Quince. If he hadn't seen the man's murderous ways himself, he would have thought the stories were a pack of lies. Now, anything anyone said, no matter how terrible, Slocum believed.

Even the one about using a splinter from the Apache's thighbone as a toothpick. A brave had been ambushed out near Columbus a day or two before the Nance family had been slaughtered like sheep. Slocum could believe it all because he had seen the crazy fire in Billy's eye when he killed the driver and shotgun messenger.

"You lookin' for him, mister?" asked the barkeep.

"Who?" Slocum knew who the bartender meant. Billy Quince was all anyone in El Paso talked about. The border town was afire with the idea of a hanging, if the town marshal got lucky enough to catch Quince.

"You got the look of a gunfighter. Heard tell half a dozen desperados have come to town to wait for Quince. Killin' him is gonna increase any man's prestige."

"Any gunman's prestige," Slocum corrected. "I'm not a gunfighter."

"Yeah, sure," the barkeep said sarcastically. His eyes

flashed to the worn ebony butt on Slocum's Colt Navy, and then to the steady hands and the cold, cold green eyes. He poured another drink and went down the bar to talk with the pair of drunken cowboys.

Slocum had seen what the barkeep meant, though. Hard men with quick hands had moved into El Paso, waiting for a chance at Billy Quince. Rumor had it that John Wesley Hardin was coming back to town just to have it out with Quince. If the fastest, orneriest gunman of them all wanted a piece of Billy's hide, that meant others would flock here to try their hands too.

Slocum realized he might not have to run Billy off. Quince might end up in a grave before he even found him.

"What's the best place for a proper young lady to stay in El Paso?" Slocum asked.

"How proper?" called the barkeep. This produced a few jeers and a round of laughter.

"Very," Slocum said in a tone that told them he wasn't looking for a whore.

"Miss Peabody's boardinghouse over on Stanton is about the best there is. Right next to the Lutheran church. Can't miss it."

This caused a few more snickers. Slocum ignored them all and left, going into the devastating desert heat outside the adobe saloon. He checked his pocket watch and then mounted his horse. Lizbeth Quince had not been on the last three stages. Perhaps she would arrive today. If she did, Slocum thought it his duty to turn her around and send her back to wherever she had come from. He rode slowly toward the Butterfield depot out at Hueco Tanks, not wanting to tire his horse. The miles vanished without him realizing it.

He sat in the shade and watched as the stagecoach rattled in, coming from the south, down Fort Davis way. Slocum couldn't help remembering the stage outside Tularosa Billy had held up. But now the driver and shotgun messenger were alive, and inside the rocking cab Slocum saw no fewer than three passengers.

One by one the passengers climbed down, but when Lizbeth Quince came out, Slocum felt his heart lodge in his throat. Billy had always boasted how lovely his sister was. Slocum had thought it was nothing but a big brother bragging on his little sister. He knew now Quince had not been a liar when he had spoken so well of Lizbeth.

The dark-haired young woman stepped down and looked around, bright blue eyes missing nothing. Not seeing her brother caused her to heave a sigh and sag a little. Slocum went to her and took off his Stetson.

"Miss Quince? Lizbeth?"

"Yes?" She looked hopeful. She blessed Slocum with a broad smile when she saw him. "You must be John. Billy's written of you so many times I feel as if I know you."

"Yes, ma'am, John Slocum."

"Please, John, call me Lizbeth. All my friends do." A cloud passed over her face as old memories robbed her of her pleasant nature. "My family did too, when I had some."

"Billy told me about your parents," Slocum said.

"Where is he? I hoped he would be here to meet me. I wrote from Kansas City two weeks ago but did not know exactly when the stagecoach would arrive."

"I figured out when you might be here and came to meet you." Slocum glanced around, wondering if Billy had shown up too. If he had, Slocum knew there would be gunplay in front of this lovely woman. Billy would think it was a fine thing to show off for his sister by killing his former partner.

"What's wrong, John? Has something happened to Billy?"

"It's mighty hot out here, Lizbeth," he said. The feel of her name on his tongue pleased him almost as much as it pained him to tell her how her brother had gone bad.

"I demand to know. I've endured so much. Has there been an accident?"

"Worse," Slocum said. He led her into the stage depot, got them both tin cups of water, and sat down on the only other chair in the depot. White-faced and anticipating the bad news, Lizbeth sank to the chair opposite and clutched the tin cup.

"If he's not injured or dead, what can be worse?"

Slocum told her.

4

Slocum was glad Lizbeth Quince was able to ride easily behind him. He had thought about how he would get the young woman from Hueco Tanks to El Paso. If he had, a buckboard or buggy would have worked fine. But he hadn't really thought she would be on that stagecoach—or any other stage.

Things worked out all right for him, though. He liked the nearness of her trim body behind him on the saddle and the way her strong arms circled his body as they bounced over the uneven desert. The horse complained as it walked, due to the double weight and the added burden of Lizbeth's two bulky, battered travel bags slung over its rump on top of the saddlebags.

"I can't believe you're talking about my brother," Lizbeth said, distraught. Her arms tightened around his waist. "He can't be out there killing men for no reason."

Slocum said nothing about Billy Quince's targets being more than armed men. Quince killed anything that moved, grown or not. That made him come to the attention of lawmen throughout the Southwest. A killer like John Wesley Hardin was given a wide berth because he was so ornery and deadly—but seldom to anyone not dealing directly with him. And Slocum had never heard even a rumor that Hardin gunned down women and children.

The next thing he expected to hear about Billy Quince was how he shot up a church during a sermon. He had violated about every other law, written and unwritten, in the West.

"I saw it with my own eyes," Slocum said. "He shot down three men and two women and never blinked an eye. Since then, he's been on a real tear, killing anything living that comes into his gunsights." He saw no way of sugar-coating the truth to spare her. Better to prepare her for the idea of seeing her brother strung up by a lynch mob.

"He's not like that," she said. "His letters never even hinted at turning so plumb mean. He wrote about the cattle and Mr. Lacey and the Lazy V and you." This last came out almost shyly.

"Lacey asked us to run down a gang of rustlers. Billy saved my life by shooting their leader. He said that was the first man he'd ever killed, and I believed him."

"He never mentioned that," Lizbeth said.

"The reward money from turning in the Paddy Patterson gang got wired to you so you could come out here," Slocum said, glad he had added some of his own reward to get Lizbeth there. He had thought it was a waste of money then. No longer.

"So that's where he got so much money. He never said."

"After we reached Tularosa, he changed fast," Slocum said. He snorted. "Patterson said the spurs Billy took off him were cursed. Might be true, for all the blood Billy's shed since then."

"Cursed?"

Slocum explained how Billy had taken the fancy silver spurs from the dying rustler. By the time he had finished the story, they reached the outskirts of what had been Franklin, Texas. Fort Bliss to the north had expanded, and now the cities on both sides of the Rio Grande called themselves El Paso.

"I heard about a decent boardinghouse for you to stay at until things work themselves out," Slocum said. "Miss Peabody's, it's called." He wound through the dusty El Paso streets, found Stanton Street, and soon saw the adobe building with a small white wooden sign outside declaring this to be "Miss Peabody's: Rooms for Gentle Ladies."

"What am I going to do, John? If Billy is running wild, as you say, what can I do?"

"He might be real docile with you. Last I saw of him, he was bouncing one way and then the other. Whenever he talked about you, he was more like the old Billy than the new."

"I cannot simply sit and wait for him, John," the dark-haired woman said firmly. "Help me track him down. That is the expression, isn't it? Track him down?" She savored the words on her lips, as if they were some new and exotic taste treat.

"Most everyone wants a piece of his hide. Billy's a clever one and not likely to be found unless it's by accident."

"Or he wants to be found," Lizbeth said.

"You're offering yourself up as bait?"

"I wouldn't put it quite so crudely, sir," she said, miffed. Lizbeth let Slocum dismount, then help her down. He pulled the two travel bags off the horse. The dun-colored horse whinnied in appreciation at the loss of such a heavy load. Slocum led the horse to a watering barrel and let it drink before pulling it away so it wouldn't bloat.

Lizbeth stood patiently, watching him and waiting without saying a word. He hefted her two travel bags and went to the door. A prim gray-haired woman in her sixties peered at him over the tops of her glasses. She turned toward Lizbeth, pointedly ignoring Slocum.

"You look tuckered out. Have you just arrived, my dear?"

"Yes, from Kansas City," Lizbeth said. Slocum let Billy's sister do the haggling over room rates as he waited. He wasn't sure what to do now. He had seen Lizbeth to a safe berth. What more did he owe her? He had decided hunting down Billy Quince was both too dangerous and not the way he wanted to spend the remainder of his life. Billy was as likely to shoot him in the back as he was to greet him. What bothered Slocum most was the notion that Billy might treat his sister the same way he had treated so many others recently.

Lizbeth didn't seem like a hothouse flower, but dealing with a cold-blooded killer instead of a loving brother was beyond her ability. Slocum wondered if dealing with Billy wasn't beyond his. Ever since he had cut down Paddy Patterson and taken his spurs, Billy Quince had changed beyond recognition.

Slocum had never shot a man in the back. If his path crossed Billy's again, he might seriously consider changing the way he operated.

He was pulled out of his reverie when Lizbeth came back to where he stood just outside Miss Peabody's.

"Let's see what we can find in the way of new clothing in town, Mr. Slocum," she said, tipping her head back slightly to show she knew Miss Peabody eavesdropped. Only proper young ladies would be permitted to stay in her boardinghouse. Slocum went along with his role as hired hand, touching the brim of his hat and escorting her from the house.

"She is very proper," Lizbeth said needlessly.

"Where do you want to go? I'll need to rent a buggy if you want to go much farther than the Plaza. As it is, that's quite a walk. I don't think Miss Peabody would approve of you riding a horse."

"Walking is fine." They strolled side by side, neither saying anything until they came to a small knot of shops along Stanton. Lizbeth idly looked in the windows at clothing and yard goods. Slocum walked slowly, trying not to stew over the inactivity. Shopping was not something he cottoned to much.

"Excuse me while I make a few purchases," Lizbeth said, ducking into a clothing store. When she came out she wore a riding outfit, her other clothes wrapped in paper and tied neatly with brown twine. "Now," she said, "I'm ready to ride. Where can I find a horse?"

"Where are you going?"

"Why, after Billy, of course," she said, as if Slocum knew exactly where the killer had gone to ground.

After making sure Miss Peabody would not rent out her room while she was gone, Lizbeth had ridden out of El Paso with him, heading north toward Tularosa, finally reaching a spot not far from Dog Canyon. Slocum and Quince had camped there on their way to working for Lacey on the Lazy V. A small stream funneled down from the higher mountains and gave cool, sweet water. Some grass grew around a pond and provided enough feed for their horses to keep them from protesting too much.

"Why are we here, John?" She looked around. For all the water, stubby junipers, and grass, this was a barren stretch fetched up against the side of the mountains.

"A hunch. Billy and I camped here before. He might come back this way."

"If he doesn't?"

Slocum shrugged. He had no idea how to track down a man moving as fast as Billy Quince, especially when Quince killed anyone likely to report him to the law. It would be like trying to rope and ride a Texas tornado.

"You're pretty smart, Slocum. You know me as good as my very own little sister."

Slocum swung around, hand resting on his six-shooter. Only force of will kept Slocum from throwing down on his former partner. He hardly recognized the man standing across the clearing half hidden in shadow as Billy Quince. He seemed heavier, more assured of himself, colder. The eyes bored into Slocum's soul like icy drills and told him how much Quince had lost since killing Paddy Patterson.

There was no hint of humanity in those twin windows to Hell.

"Billy!" Lizbeth ran to her brother and threw her arms around him, hugging him close. Slocum watched for any sign that the man might turn on his sister. Billy seemed genuinely pleased to see Lizbeth again. Then the pleasure faded and a mask of disdain replaced it, as if Billy Quince could hardly bear to be in the company of anyone this callow.

Quince pushed Lizbeth to one side and squared off, gaze fixed on Slocum.

"This here's my old partner, but I think he's turned bounty hunter, little sister. I think he's come after me for the reward. How much is it now, John? How bad does the law want me? I'd heard the federal marshal was offering a full thousand dollars for me."

"Billy, you're joking. Tell me you haven't done all those terrible things!" exclaimed Lizbeth. He pushed the dark-haired woman out of the way so he could keep Slocum fixed in his field of vision.

"I owe you plenty. And I'm no bounty hunter," Slocum said in a level voice. "Your sister wanted to see you after you didn't show up to meet her at the stage depot."

"But you just happened by, is that it, John? You makin' time with my little sister? You violate her?" The edge to Billy Quince's voice dropped the desert temperature ten degrees.

"Billy!" Lizbeth was trying to reason with her brother, but Slocum saw the madness closing around Quince like a shroud. Any hint of the old Billy he had called partner vanished entirely as the man's right hand began twitching. He was getting ready to draw, whether Slocum did or not.

"I've been nothing but a gentleman toward her," Slocum said, "but I don't reckon you'd believe anything I said."

"Reckon not," Billy said. "You ready to meet your maker, Slocum? I've killed danged near twenty men."

"How many women and children?"

"I don't count them. Mexicans or niggers either."

"Billy, how dare you!" Lizbeth avoided his outstretched arm and positioned herself directly in front of him. "You know better than to talk like that. And I can't hardly believe you *think* like that too!"

Slocum watched for Quince's hand to start moving for his six-gun. Somehow, Lizbeth still had a bit of influence over him. His lips curled in a sneer; then he pushed her away and stalked off. Slocum considered how much easier his life would be if he shot Billy Quince in the back. He knew Quince had murdered wantonly, had taken the lives of women without any cause.

If he killed Quince he might even get a hefty reward. Marshal Hanssen had hinted that the money on Quince's head was building. Slocum ought to have gunned Quince down. But he didn't.

The pounding of hooves told him that Quince was high-tailing it away, heading north, possibly into the malpais north of Tularosa and the Valley of Fires.

"He just rode off, John. He . . . that didn't look like my brother at all."

"You saying he's not Billy Quince?" Slocum was surprised at this.

"No, he's my Billy. But he's so different! Did you hear the anger in his voice? He's learned to hate."

"He's learned more than that," Slocum said. "He's learned to enjoy killing."

Lizbeth came to him, and buried her face into his shoulder. He felt wetness from her tears soaking into his dusty shirt. Her entire body shook as she tried to keep from sobbing. Slocum held her close, not sure what else he could do until she looked up, her blue eyes moist and her lips trembling.

He wasn't quite certain what was happening until she

kissed him. The touch of her lips on his was tentative at first; then Lizbeth's passion mounted. She clung to him hard. He felt her firm young breasts crushing into his body. Slocum was never quite sure what happened, but they moved around as if they were waltzing in some grand ballroom, unheard music directing their every movement. All the while they kissed, turning and twisting, their hands roved over each other's bodies until both were naked to the waist.

Slocum pulled back a little and stared at Lizbeth's white breasts. His mouth went dry then.

"We shouldn't—" he began.

"We should," Lizbeth insisted. She took his hand and moved it to her left breast, then moved it so his palm crushed down on her chest. She closed her eyes and moaned softly. "I need you, John. Don't deny me."

"Deny you?" He almost laughed. He had lusted for her from the moment he saw her. Riding to El Paso had been a chore for him, her arms circling his waist, her body pressing into his, but he had been nothing but a gentleman.

He wasn't going to deny her—or his own sexual desires.

Slocum kissed her lips and cheeks and eyes and nibbled at her shell-like ears, and then moved down her arching throat until he ended up with his face buried between her breasts. Lizbeth made small animal noises, but did not move away. If anything, she spurred him on.

They sank to the grass and rolled over and over. Somehow, he lifted her skirts and exposed paradise. His hand moved between her thighs and found the crinkly-furred thatch and the dampness within. She gasped as his finger entered her most intimate recess. Lizbeth's legs parted and she reached out to him.

"Yes, John, yes. I need you so." Her voice combined longing and such anguish it made Slocum ache just hearing it. He could not deny her, even if he wanted.

He moved between her upraised knees, his manhood aching with need. It brushed over her thatched triangle and then plunged past her nether lips. One instant he was out in the cold. The next he was totally surrounded by clinging, moist female flesh. She sucked in her breath, and he thought she was going to crush him flat. Strong female muscles all around his hardness squeezed down on him and promised so much more pleasure.

Slocum had to catch his breath. Sweat poured down his face and dripped onto Lizbeth's naked chest, tickling and stimulating. He smiled at her as he slowly rotated his hips, stirring himself around in her tightness like a spoon in a bowl. Feeling the tensions within his own body mount, Slocum paused to recover until his loins demanded more. He began stroking, slowly at first and then faster and faster. Lizbeth gasped and moaned and thrashed about under him. He looked down into her lovely face and saw confusion and lust and the need to forget. His hips moved faster and carnal heat mounted until he was no longer able to contain himself.

Lizbeth cried out as he spilled his seed. He continued pumping until he was exhausted. Slocum sank down beside her on the ground. Their arms intertwined and she pulled him closer.

"Reckon your brother had more insight than I credited him with," Slocum said.

"You didn't violate me," Lizbeth said firmly. "That implies taking me against my will. Was there any point where you thought I wasn't wholeheartedly cooperating?" She rolled slightly so she could look directly at him.

"No," Slocum admitted. Lizbeth was an intelligent woman able to make her own decisions, and she had decided that Slocum had what she needed right now.

He felt her fingers stroking over his belly and working lower. She caught at his flaccid organ and began squeezing, coaxing him into readiness again. Lizbeth stroked slowly, gently. Her mouth breath against his chest and the smell of her hair and the feel of her nakedness against his excited him as much as her hand.

Then she unexpectedly said, "I didn't see the spurs Billy wore. He took them off the rustler he killed?"

"The spurs," Slocum said. "That's quite a story."

"Again. Tell me again," she urged. Slocum wasn't sure he was up to it, but she convinced him.

5

"There must be someone else who knows," Lizbeth Quince said. She frowned and bit at her thumb, thinking hard about everything Slocum had said.

"The only others who might know are the rest of Patterson's gang. We only drilled three of them. There had to be a couple more," Slocum said. He didn't want to go on a wild-goose chase, but he felt he owed something to Lizbeth—and to her brother. He couldn't ride off and leave her alone in the middle of the New Mexican desert. Summer grilled the sand and made hunting difficult. Even the jackrabbits had taken to their burrows and refused to poke up their long-eared heads.

"Where are they?"

"I suppose the sheriff in Tularosa might know. Or maybe Marshal Hanssen from up in Santa Fe."

"Let's not wait about then," she said with determination. "I want to find out all I can about these spurs. That has to be the reason Billy is acting so strangely."

Slocum hesitated to say anything. Spurs didn't turn a man into a kill-crazed fool. Something had snapped inside Billy Quince to make him the murderer he was. Slocum had never seen it in the months they had ridden together, and that bothered him. He was usually a better judge of character, but he had to admit he sometimes made mistakes. In Billy's case, it was almost a deadly one.

"If your friendship with Billy means anything, John, you must try to help him." The way her blue eyes pinned him like a bug with a needle through its abdomen got to Slocum.

"I owe him, but thinking silver spurs are the cause of all this woe, well, that's plumb crazy."

"You might say so, but I believe differently," she said almost primly. "I have seen fortune tellers use a deck of the tarot to predict the future. There is a way of observing the heavens and finding movements of the celestial orbs to determine the future also."

"Astrology," Slocum said.

"You have heard of it," she said, almost relieved.

"I rode with a medicine show for a spell," Slocum said. "They sold snake oil and lies. Part of it was done with cards, the rest by invoking the movements of the stars."

"You don't believe," Lizbeth said sadly.

"I believe your brother's six-shooter is going to be his death. He's gotten faster on the draw, but there are men riding here in the West who could kill him before breakfast and not even work up a sweat." Slocum wasn't afraid of John Wesley Hardin, but he knew he ought to be. If it came down to riding down a side street or sharing the main road with Hardin, Slocum knew which he would take. He was no coward. He wasn't a fool either. Mad dogs and mad-dog killers were breeds unto themselves. To think he could go up against either one and win was folly.

"Do you believe Billy is heading back to Tularosa?" Lizbeth was nothing if not determined.

"Might be," Slocum allowed. They got their gear together and rode on, Lizbeth humming to herself and Slocum cursing the day he was born.

"You don't get no reward for either of them rustlers," the sheriff said testily. "Me and Deputy Holbrook brung 'em in all by ourselves."

"They rode with Paddy Patterson?" asked Slocum.

"Course they did. Why else would we be tryin' them, then hangin' 'em?" The sheriff glared at Slocum as if he was worried the reward might slip through his fingers.

"I don't have any claim on the reward, Sheriff," Slocum said. He wished he could talk to the federal marshal out of Santa Fe. Hanssen was a more reasonable man—and better paid. A sheriff in Tularosa might not make twenty dollars a month. Even a small reward would look mighty fine to him.

"All you want is to talk to 'em? 'Bout what?"

"That's personal, Sheriff," Lizbeth said. The lawman couldn't keep his eyes off her, Slocum saw. The sheriff ran his dirty hands up and down his jeans, as if he couldn't keep his hands off her either.

"Go on. Five minutes. No more."

Slocum and Lizbeth went into the back of the Tularosa calaboose. The single cell was nothing but an iron cage. Breaking out would take more effort than simply shooting whoever tended the key to the massive lock on the door.

Two men glanced up, then exchanged looks. Neither moved as Slocum went closer.

"Paddy Patterson," he said. "Where'd he get the silver spurs he wore?"

"Not even a 'how are you doing?' or 'pleased to make your acquaintance'?" asked the larger of the two men. The other laughed and lounged back on his narrow bunk. There were only boards on it—no mattress. He didn't seem to mind.

"Please," Lizbeth pleaded. "We need to know about the spurs."

"Little lady, if you'd come closer, I'll let you know about something more fun than those damn spurs."

Lizbeth stiffened in indignation. Before she could speak, Slocum said, "You boys might rot in here—unless they string you up first."

"So? What are you tellin' us we don't know already?"
Both rustlers eyed him suspiciously now.

"Tell me what I want to know and there might just be
a way out of here. Before your trial tomorrow."

"Tomorrow! Why that lyin' sack of cow flop said the
circuit judge wasn't due for another month!"

Slocum motioned Lizbeth to silence. She objected to his
outrageous lying, but Slocum knew he wasn't likely to get
information from these two any other way. They had to be
scared into talking, and nothing much besides having a
noose tightened around their necks was likely to do the
trick.

"That all you want to know? Not where Paddy hid the
loot?"

"The spurs," Lizbeth said, betraying her eagerness.

The big man snorted in contempt. "Never saw what
Paddy liked about them spurs. Sure, they was fancy, but it
was more that he took 'em off the Rio Kid than anything
else."

"Backshootin' son of a bitch," grumbled the other man.
"Never saw anyone more inclined to shotgun you when
you wasn't lookin'."

"I never heard of the Rio Kid," Slocum said.

"Came up from Mexico. Hated Mexicans and killed
every one he come across," said the other outlaw. "Had
somethin' to do with when he was a kid they killed his
family."

"The spurs," Slocum prompted. "What about them?"

"Paddy took 'em off the Kid when he was sleepin'.
Leastways, that's my guess how he got them. Paddy was
never man enough to face a gunslick like the Kid."

"Where did this Rio Kid get the spurs?" asked Lizbeth.

"Heard tell he stole them from a *brujo* down in Mexico."

"*Brujo?*" Lizbeth frowned, unfamiliar with the term.

"A Mexican sorcerer. An old man who cast spells and
turned people into bats or something like that. All Mexicans

are a superstitious lot. No tellin' where the *brujo* got the spurs.''

"Likely stole them, just like the Rio Kid and Paddy,'' said the other rustler. They both laughed at this.

"Or maybe the Rio Kid killed somebody the *brujo* cottoned to and he put a curse on the spurs, knowin' they'd be stolen,'' declared the larger of the two prisoners. "Seems like fittin' justice, havin' a man like the Kid steal cursed spurs.''

"Come on,'' Slocum said to Lizbeth. "We've heard enough.''

"Hey, when you bustin' us out of here?''

Slocum paused, looked around, then said, "When you tell us the truth.''

"That *was* the God's truth! The Rio Kid got the spurs from the *brujo*!''

Slocum pushed Lizbeth from the jailhouse and into the street. He didn't even bother thanking the sheriff. The lawman was already glaring at him as if Slocum had finally figured out how to steal the reward. Slocum didn't want him getting suspicious and asking around. He might just find another reward to collect—this one on Slocum's head.

"John, that explains it all,'' Lizbeth said. "The spirit of this practitioner of native voodoo has infused the spurs and that is what is making Billy into a killer.''

Slocum shook his head to clear it. He hardly believed Lizbeth was so intent on this.

"It all makes sense,'' the lovely dark-haired woman insisted. "The curse was placed on the spurs and whoever wears them is similarly cursed.''

"Sure, the Rio Kid and Paddy Patterson were law-abiding citizens driven crazy by the curse.'' Slocum didn't believe this for an instant. There were two kinds of men: predators and prey. Both the Rio Kid and Paddy Patterson sounded like they'd been predators all their lives. The spurs did nothing to them their basic ornery natures hadn't already done.

But he still had trouble explaining why Billy had snapped the way he had.

"The Rio Kid is the one to ask," she said. "That horrible man back there in jail did say Paddy Patterson had stolen the spurs from him."

"You want to track down a man with the personality of a sidewinder and ask him how he lost a pair of spurs?" Slocum bit back the rest of his denunciation of this crackbrained idea. The Rio Kid would want one thing only from a woman as lovely as Lizbeth Quince. And she wasn't likely to get more than a passel of bad memories—or just end up dead.

"Yes, of course. How difficult can it be?"

"Never heard of this owlhoot till now," Slocum said. He looked up and down the alkali-dust streets of Tularosa, and wondered if he ought to go back into the sheriff's office and ask. Slocum heaved a sigh, left Lizbeth outside, and in a few minutes returned. He wasn't sure if he was pleased at what he had learned.

"Well?" she demanded. The dark-haired woman pushed a strand of hair from her bright eyes. She seemed so innocent, so eager.

"Might be down at Fort Davis or even over at Fort Griffin."

"I came through Fort Davis and did not hear of such a desperado," she said.

While this was hardly any indication of the Kid's whereabouts, Slocum suspected she was right. Slocum had been to Fort Griffin and didn't like the place much. It stood on a hill about a half mile from the Clear Fork in the Brazos River and attracted some of the meanest outlaws in the West. Doc Holliday had spent a fair amount of time there, as had John Wesley Hardin—and apparently, the Rio Kid.

They left for Fort Griffin at dawn.

• • •

"This isn't doing much running down your brother," Slocum said, staring up at the fort. A sutler's store made from sod at the bottom of the hill had a couple of sheep grazing on the roof. Other buildings scattered about told of the sporadic trade from the fort. A dozen saloons lined what passed for a street. At the moment, it was baked harder than slate. Come the rains, it would turn into knee-deep mud. That kind of summed up the entire community, as Slocum saw it.

"We need to know what we are up against, John. I've told you, the key to Billy's behavior is locked in those silver spurs."

Slocum shook his head sadly. By now her brother probably had tangled with a man faster or sneakier and was lying in a shallow grave—if he was lucky. If Quince had tried to rob another stagecoach, he might be drawing flies and buzzards alongside some lonely road. No shotgun messenger or coach driver worth his salt would take the time to bury a fallen highwayman.

"When we find the Rio Kid, let me do the talking," Slocum said. "Truth to tell, I'd feel a sight better if he didn't even set eyes on you." Even after the long trip across West Texas, the woman was still about the prettiest thing John Slocum had ever seen. They had spent some pleasant nights, some passionate ones, and always he enjoyed her company. That satisfaction would wear mighty thin if she tried to deal directly with a man like the Rio Kid.

Slocum didn't know him—or much about him. That didn't matter. Slocum had seen too many killers in his day not to be able to identify the Rio Kid immediately. Slocum didn't figure to find him in church either. From the look of the saloons, many only canvas tents, a few two stories tall with cribs upstairs for the soiled doves and their customers—most of those made of precious wood planks and sod—he had a considerable amount of hunting ahead of him in places where Lizbeth would be stared at.

These were not places a decent woman went. Ever.

"We'll camp outside town, out on the flats," Slocum said. "You go find a spot, and I'll join you when I can."

"You're going into the saloons, aren't you?" Lizbeth asked, a tone of disappointment cutting like a knife.

"That's where I'll find the Rio Kid," Slocum said.

"Very well. I suppose I knew it wouldn't be easy to find such a desperate man."

Slocum knew that was about as far from the truth as she could get, but did not correct her. The people in a town, even one as rough-and-tumble as Fort Griffin, would boast and whisper about any notorious gunfighter coming through. It was about all they had to occupy their time, other than drinking, gambling, and whoring.

Slocum set off on foot to get the lay of the land. It had been years since he had come this way, but Fort Griffin hadn't changed one whit. He saw two dead horses and a dog that was well nigh dead in the street. No one cared enough to move them or the flies accumulating on their stinking carcasses. The stench from garbage was incredible where it was tossed out the back doors. It made Slocum long for the clean, dry desert air of West Texas again.

Everything about Fort Griffin made him long to be on the trail. He went into a likely-looking saloon and looked around. A cracked mirror behind the long polished wood bar needed replacing. The floorboards were warped, making walking difficult enough sober. For those who had imbibed too much, just getting out of the saloon would be a chore.

He bellied up to the bar and waited for the barkeep to notice him.

"Whiskey," he said, dropping a dime on the counter. It vanished and was replaced with a shot glass of weak-looking whiskey. His first sip about knocked him to the floor.

"Good stuff, ain't it?" asked the bartender. "My own recipe."

"Good," Slocum said, trying to keep from coughing. He drank in silence a while, then struck up a conversation with the barkeep.

"Naw, I ain't been in town too long," the barkeep declared. "Not more than six months. 'Fore that I was up in Abilene. Cow towns are dyin', they are. I decided to follow some of the gamblers to see if this place was as tough as they said. It is."

"Reckon so, with the likes of the Rio Kid hanging out here," Slocum said. This produced a chuckle.

"What's so funny?" Slocum asked.

"The Rio Kid, that's what. He blowed into town like he was the fastest gun in the West, then went and got himself gutshot while he was sleepin'. Strange 'bout that, though."

"What's so strange about a man like that being shot?" asked Slocum, feeling a load lift from him. The Rio Kid was long dead from the sound of it. That meant he didn't have to find out about the spurs. But it also presented a problem in ever finding out who had fashioned the spurs.

"I saw it, the whole danged robbery and murder. Paddy Patterson done the deed. He tried to pry loose the Kid's spurs while he was passed out over in that corner." He pointed to the far corner of the saloon. "The Rio Kid came to and put up a fight, but not much of one, considerin' his reputation."

"Paddy Patterson shot him for the spurs?"

"That's the way I saw it. And as he lay in his own blood, a slug in his gut, the Kid was laughin' like he'd jist heard the best joke in the world."

Slocum considered this for a moment. "Was that before or after Patterson got the spurs?"

The barkeep scratched his stubbled chin as he thought. "Now that I think on it, it was after the spurs was stolen. Cain't imagine what was goin' on in the Kid's head, but he was falling-down drunk."

Slocum frowned. The Rio Kid laughed when Paddy Patterson stole his spurs, though he had a bullet in the belly.

"The Kid's dead?"

"The field north of town's full of men like him. No family, no friends, no one even willing to drink a quart of hooch and piss on the grave. Might have been a marker put up to celebrate his passin', but I kinda doubt it." The barkeep squinted a little at Slocum, then asked, "You a friend of his?"

"The Rio Kid didn't have any friends," Slocum said.

"Then you're a friend of Paddy Patterson?"

"My partner and I sent him to the promised land."

"Damnation. If I go on losin' customers like that, I might have to close the place." The barkeep laughed and moved on to deal with a pair of rowdy cavalry privates at the far side of the saloon.

Slocum finished his firewater and left, walking slowly toward the north end of the street. He remembered a potter's field in this direction. A hundred yards beyond a whorehouse he found the cemetery looking just as it had before, except it had more graves.

Wandering up and down, checking occasional crosses or markers with names scratched into rock, he was about ready to give up when he came to a grave. Slocum couldn't rightly tell, but it looked to be at least three months old from the way the dirt had packed down. A simple cross with the inscription "Rio Kid—damn you to Hell" had been driven into the ground. The wood on the cross was starting to rot. This was the only clue Slocum had to the age of the grave.

"You died with your boots on—but not with your spurs," he said softly. Slocum couldn't help wondering if in fact the fancy silver Spanish spurs Paddy Patterson had coveted might not be the cause of Billy Quince's sudden turn of character.

He shook his head at such a sorry notion, turned, and left the Rio Kid to molder in peace for the rest of eternity.

Slocum had to figure out what to tell Lizbeth now that it was apparent they weren't going to learn any more about the spurs.

Those damned spurs.

6

"Dead end," Slocum said resolutely. He leaned back against his bedroll, propped up on his elbows, and watched how Lizbeth Quince took the news. "The Rio Kid has been dead for months. The best I can tell, Paddy Patterson actually killed him. Shot him while he was sleeping, then stole his spurs."

"And the Kid laughed after Paddy Patterson shot him," she said firmly. "I spoke with several women in Fort Griffin and heard that part of the story too. Everyone knows it, John, everyone! The Rio Kid knew what Patterson was getting himself into and was happy to be rid of the spurs, even if it meant he would burn in Hell forever. That must mean whoever wears them cannot take them off or get rid of them unless they die."

"It's a matter of wanting," Slocum said tiredly. "You want flashing silver spurs that attract the attention of any cowboy who sees them, you wear them. You don't want attention like that, you take them off. Paddy Patterson was a thief and killer. So was the Rio Kid, from all accounts. There's no honor among thieves. The spurs were a badge of how vicious a killer he was, that's all."

It was as if Lizbeth never heard him. She stood and paced back and forth on the far side of the small campfire.

Several times she started to speak, then clamped her mouth shut. Finally she came to a conclusion on the matter. Even before she spoke her mind, Slocum knew he wasn't going to like it.

"We go back to El Paso," she said in her determined fashion. "Billy seems to consider that home now. We find him and wrestle him down and get rid of the spurs for him. That might be the only way to save him from himself."

"You're still thinking the spurs are causing his killing spree?" Slocum knew better than to argue with her, but this was too absurd for words. He couldn't even come up with a decent argument that would convince her of how dumb it sounded.

"It all fits, John." She sank down and warmed her hands near the fire. Her blue eyes gleamed like sapphires in the night. "The Rio Kid went on a killing spree when he donned the spurs. Paddy Patterson stole them off a man he had shot, then did the same thing the Kid had. Billy got the spurs, and look what he's doing!"

Slocum didn't bother pointing out that both the Rio Kid and Patterson had been owlhoots before they put on the fancy Mexican spurs. Facts wouldn't sway her. He sighed, lay back, and stared at the diamond-hard stars above, the light occasionally hidden by fluffy dark clouds blowing across the prairie sky. He would see her back to El Paso and on her way to San Francisco or wherever she wanted to go. Then he would ride his own trail. It had been years since he had been to the Dakotas. He had nothing but fond memories of Fargo. Seldom had he seen a place with higher-stakes poker games and more men who didn't know the odds of drawing to inside straights.

With thoughts of distant horizons lapping at the edges of his mind, Slocum fell asleep.

"Miss Peabody wasn't too pleased to see you again," Slocum observed. The old woman had glared at him when they rode up, and had spoken to Lizbeth in short, snippy sentences when the dark-haired woman obviously intended to claim her room again. Sitting now in the cool inner patio of the adobe boardinghouse afforded privacy—but not too much since the building circled them, affording any number of places where the owner could spy on them.

None of that mattered to Slocum. He had seen Lizbeth back to El Paso from Fort Griffin. It was time for them to part company, though Slocum would miss her a powerful lot. Lizbeth had spirit, intelligence, and had proven a quick study learning how to live on the trail. She had become skilled enough to bag a rabbit for dinner, fix the cooking fire, and then roast the game to a turn.

"I doubt we'll have long to wait for Billy." She sounded dour. She sat on the bench beside him, clutching a wad of newsprint so hard she tore a few pages under her fingers.

"Why do you say that?" Slocum asked.

He took the newspaper Lizbeth handed him. Billy Quince had made the headlines in a border town not often shocked by criminal deeds. Slocum read the colorful account of how Billy had single-handedly robbed a bank near Fort Bliss, leaving behind three dead and two wounded. All in the bank would have been dead if he hadn't run out of ammunition.

Slocum shook his head in disbelief at what he read. Billy had robbed a bank carrying only a single pistol and a shotgun—and no spare ammo. He had walked in, shotgunned the two surprised guards, then used his six-shooter on a teller before emptying the bank vault of almost five hundred dollars. On his way out he had shot two customers, one already inside the bank lobby and the other just entering to do some business.

"This is plumb crazy," Slocum said.

"The spurs, John. It's the spurs he took."

"That's as good a reason as any. He didn't plan this," Slocum guessed. "He saw the bank, and then and there took it into his head to rob it. So he walked in and just did it."

The sheer stupidity of the robbery bothered Slocum the most. Billy hadn't wanted the money. He had wanted people to kill. That was the only—the best—explanation for such behavior. Quince had been careful when he had ridden with Slocum. The man had taken no unnecessary chances, had always played it safe.

Before.

Slocum kept reading, and found a story relating to something Billy Quince had done earlier in the week. Slocum was even more amazed. Billy had called out a local gunman of some minor reputation. They had gone out in the street and shot at each other until the gunman caught one of Billy's slugs in his head. The wound hadn't killed him, but had left him comatose. The doctor tending the gunman said he doubted the man would ever regain consciousness, and if he did he would be little, more than an idiot.

Slocum folded the *El Paso Daily Times* and handed it back to Lizbeth. He hardly knew what to say.

"So how do we find him? He won't return to that watering hole we saw him at before, will he, John?"

"He's moving into new territory," Slocum said, not referring to the countryside. Billy was learning what it felt like to be a killer. Something in the act of spilling blood thrilled him. Once he had tasted that forbidden pleasure, there was no turning back for him. Slocum had seen too much killing, and it still bothered him. Some men deserved to die, others didn't. But death always brought up a strong emotion of revenge or loss in Slocum.

Billy felt only pleasure at death now. Slocum was sure of that. And murdering wasn't a pleasure the man could ever get enough of, until he was killed someday soon.

"Then we must go after him," Lizbeth said.

"There's no point. Lizbeth, you ought to move on, get on with your life, find someplace where you can forget about your brother." Slocum looked up, and saw Miss Peabody frowning as she spied on them from a nearby doorway. She flounced off when Slocum met her stare, challenging her to continue her eavesdropping.

"He's my brother," Lizbeth said. "He's the only blood kin I have left. John, you don't know what that's like."

He knew, but said nothing. There was no convincing her. In her way, Lizbeth was just like her brother. She got an idea in her head and nothing could shake it loose.

"I need your help. Please, John. Please," she pleaded.

"He's got a whale of a reward on his head. That makes him the target for everyone carrying a gun in West Texas. And even men who would never think of plugging someone will be willing to put Billy Quince into a shallow grave, if only to protect themselves and their families. A man who makes such a point of killing women and children has no friends anywhere."

"All the more reason to get to him first and stop him, John."

"I might have to shoot him. Would you want to be there to see that?"

Lizbeth swallowed hard. "It won't come to that. There's got to be some way of tracking Billy down."

Slocum couldn't figure what it was. Billy jumped around like a flea on a hot griddle, no destination in mind. He killed and moved on to find more victims, and that was all the ambition he had now.

"What if the Rio Kid had a family?" asked Lizbeth. "A wife perhaps. A sister or brother or mother. Can we find out and ask?"

"Ask what?" Slocum was past figuring out what went on in Lizbeth's head.

"Ask if there is some way of getting rid of the curse. If we can't find Billy and take the spurs from him, we might find someone who can remove the curse. But we have to know what the curse is." Lizbeth sounded so earnest she convinced Slocum. Almost.

"It wouldn't do any good."

"John, do this for me. This one last thing. You don't owe me, but you do owe Billy. Please."

Slocum cursed himself for a fool and went to ask a few questions around El Paso.

The adobe building had crumbled and the roof probably leaked—if it ever rained. The hot, dusty day told Slocum the occupant of the building across the Rio Grande in the Mexican part of El Paso del Norte had little to worry about any time soon.

"The Rio Kid's wife lives here?" asked Lizbeth.

"Gunfighters' wives don't live too well," Slocum observed, dismounting. Lizbeth slid from the saddle and looked around nervously, as if someone might rush up to steal her horse. Slocum felt safer here than he did in most of the El Paso saloons.

A small woman with short, straight black hair pushed aside a serape hanging down to serve as a door. Dark eyes fixed on Slocum. He couldn't read what was going on behind those eyes, but he doubted it was too congenial toward him.

"Buenos dias," he greeted.

"I speak English," she said, for the first time eyeing Lizbeth.

"We're looking for the wife of the Rio Kid," Lizbeth said, the words tumbling out.

"He's dead. Why do you want to know about him? There is no longer the reward on his head." The woman spat. The greedy dirt sucked up the moisture almost instantly.

"The silver spurs," Lizbeth said anxiously. "My brother has the spurs. He took them from the man who killed your husband."

The woman's response surprised Slocum. Shock registered on her impassive face and her eyes burned with a passion now that hadn't been present even a few seconds earlier. She motioned Lizbeth and Slocum into her house. Slocum ducked as he entered the low door. Inside was neat, if dusty. With a dirt floor, there wasn't much chance of keeping the dust down, but the plain, crude furnishings were as well kept as they could be. She didn't live lavishly, but did live adequately compared with others nearby.

"Sit," the woman said.

Lizbeth sank into the room's single chair. Slocum stood behind her. The woman poured blue-and-white ceramic cups of water for them. Slocum took his and downed it. Lizbeth was too intent on finding out about the spurs to even pick up her cup.

"How can the curse be lifted? We know all about it."

"All?" The woman laughed. "You know *all* about it? You know nothing."

"Then tell us," Slocum said.

"Joseph was not a nice man. To me, he was always loving, but others?" She shook her head. "He was a killer. He stole spurs made for Don Jaime Villalobos of Cuernavaca by a Yaqui *brujo*. The spurs were supposed to protect Don Jaime."

"But the Rio Kid stole them?"

"He stole them from the servant Don Jaime sent to carry them back to the hacienda," the woman said. "Don Jaime was furious. The Yaqui reversed the curse so it no longer protects, it drives the wearer mad." She made a spinning motion next to her head with her forefinger.

"So your Joseph started killing like a madman?" asked Lizbeth.

"He was always the killer. But he no longer thought when he did it. Joe killed anything and everyone. Even to me, he became an animal. I threw him out, saying I wanted no more to do with him. Why did I need him? He would not marry me in a church but he always claimed me as his own."

"You're lucky he didn't kill you," Slocum said.

She shrugged. "He would have left his *cojones* behind if he had tried. He knew this." She smiled almost sadly. "There still the love for me inside him then. After he left?" She shook her head. "I heard the tales."

"How do we reverse the curse? Where's the Yaqui *brujo*?"

"Dead," the woman said. "Long dead. So is Don Jaime. My Joseph killed them all. Their curse on him became a curse on them. Justice." She spat again.

"Who else can lift the curse?" asked Lizbeth.

"No one. Only the *brujo* casting the curse can remove it. And he is dead. No one can stop the spurs from infesting with craziness the mind of whoever wears them. He will kill and kill and kill until someone kills him. That is the true curse."

"The only way of stopping Billy is for him to die?" Lizbeth spoke in a low, choked voice.

"He is your husband?"

"My brother."

"Prepare his grave. That is all you can do for him."

"No! I—"

"Lizbeth, come on," Slocum said, taking her arm and pulling her from the chair. "There's nothing we can do here." He wondered if everyone else had gone insane but him. All this wild talk of *brujos* and curses and outraged *patrónes* served no purpose. Men were dead, not from a curse but from six-shooters aimed by stone killers.

"You will never convince him to take off the spurs," the woman said. "I know. I spoke with my Joseph and he would not do it, though he knew they drove him. That is part of the curse also."

Slocum pushed Lizbeth from the adobe and toward their horses.

"John, there is so much more I need to learn from her! We've got to go back."

"This is the end of the trail. If you swallowed this preposterous story hook, line, and sinker, there's nothing you can do for your brother. If the spurs are making him kill anyone he sees, you heard her say there's no way to stop the curse. And if I'm right, that Billy is killing for some other reason, nothing you do to the spurs will matter. Either way, he's lost.''

"No!"

They rode back across the Rio Grande, each lost in their own thoughts. Slocum reckoned it was time to move on, but leaving Lizbeth would be hard with her so distraught. He had to do it because staying with her only fostered false hope that something could be done to help her brother.

7

"I don't have a whole lot of money," Slocum said, "but I'll see to getting you a ticket to wherever you want to go. You can get out to San Francisco on the railroad or return to Kansas City and—"

"I won't leave Billy," Lizbeth Quince said firmly. "He's my only kin now that my parents upped and died. It's not in me to turn my back on anyone needing help, much less Billy."

"It's easy to see why he thought the world of you," Slocum said. "That was before he went loco."

"The spurs, John," she insisted. Lizbeth ran her hands through her long, dark hair in a gesture that told of her frustration, with him for not believing, with Billy, with everything. "The spurs are making him act this way. I . . . I don't know what I am going to do when we get the spurs away from him, though. He has committed some terrible crimes, but it wasn't his fault. The curse made him—"

"There isn't a curse," Slocum said, "but you are right about one thing. If he's caught, he'll stand trial for about the worst things a man can do out West. It'll be best if he does swing for them. I don't know how any man could bear up under the guilt of killing women and children like he's done."

Slocum doubted Billy Quince would ever stand trial. Capturing him would be like trying to wrestle a grizzly to submission. If he didn't kill you trying to get away, he'd die to keep from being lassoed and put into a cage. Billy was headed for a grave. There was no other end Slocum could see for this reign of killing and robbery.

"You refuse to help me?" Lizbeth held back tears. Her lower lip quivered and she seemed on the point of exploding. A few quick breaths calmed her enough to continue without crying. "We've come so close to saving him, John. So close. You'd ride away now?"

"I don't see that we're close to finding him at all," he said honestly. "Billy's somewhere in West Texas or New Mexico Territory. That's a mighty big stretch of emptiness, and he rides mighty fast. We had a chance at that campsite outside Dog Canyon and he got away. I don't think there'll be another chance to even talk to him, much less catch him."

"You've done so much for us, John. More than I could have expected from a total stranger and someone who's not kinfolk. I reckon I ought to thank you. I promise not to think poorly of you for abandoning Billy and me like this."

Slocum knew when he was being played with, and it made him angry. Lizbeth tried to use the emotional strings tied to his heart and honor to bind him. It wouldn't work this time. He had done what he could for both his partner and his partner's sister. Anything more was a fool's errand and a waste of time. It might even be deadly. The way Billy had become, it might pleasure him to put a bullet in an old friend's back. Slocum didn't even want to think what Quince might do to his sister. He had shown a taste for killing women. Slocum didn't doubt Quince had also raped along the way.

"Let it be. Don't try to track him down alone," Slocum said. "If you are right about the spurs being cursed, he's too dangerous for you to deal with. If I'm right and he's just turned bad, he's *still* too dangerous."

"You know me better than that. I can't walk away now," Lizbeth said.

"Didn't think so." Slocum watched as she dismounted in front of Miss Peabody's boardinghouse. Lizbeth didn't even look back as she went into the house. Heaving a sigh of resignation, Slocum swung his horse around and rode down Stanton Street, wondering where he ought to head. He still had a job with the Lazy V, although he hadn't stopped Billy Quince as Lacey had wanted. Smitty wouldn't take kindly to him showing up again, and he wondered what the other cowboys would think. Probably that he had let Billy get away intentionally. That wouldn't help his standing in their eyes, not at all.

He had once considered Denver after finishing the season with the Lazy V. That seemed a foolish dream now. In his mind Denver became a stopover as he made his way to the Dakotas. The Dakotas were as far from the tornado produced by Billy Quince as he could get. Still, riding up the Jornado del Muerto in the middle of summer didn't appeal much to him. The Rio Grande was either dry or just muddy in patches and wouldn't give enough water for his horse—or him.

"Been to Fort Griffin," he said to himself. He didn't like the fort or the town around it any better than he had when he had seen it the last time years back. Mexico started to appeal more and more to him. A bottle of tequila and a willing *señorita* and a chance to take a siesta in the hot afternoon sun seemed perfect.

He turned his horse toward the Rio Grande and rode slowly until he was at the riverbank again. Reining in, he thought of how he and Lizbeth had crossed to talk to the Rio Kid's widow such a short time before. Then other things came to him. Slocum turned his pony's face and rode back toward the boardinghouse. He had to tell Lizbeth good-bye properly. It wasn't in him to let her forge ahead on her own. He didn't have much money, but he'd give it to her so she could leave El Paso—or continue the futile hunt for her brother. It would be her decision.

Slocum slowed and stared at the side of the boarding-house. A half-dozen horses were tethered there that hadn't been when he'd ridden out not fifteen minutes earlier. At first he thought it might be Billy and a gang; then logic brought out the obvious problem with that answer. Billy wasn't out recruiting a gang. He was on a one-man killing spree. Nobody in his right mind would ride with a man as likely to shoot him in the back as talk to him.

Unless that man was as crazy as Billy Quince. That Billy might have found five others willing to shed blood for the sheer thrill of it made Slocum uneasy.

He dismounted and walked to the horses. They were all tuckered out. Whoever rode them had put quite a few miles on the animals recently. Flecks of lather showed how difficult their trip in the hot desert sun had been and how much the horses needed water, grain, and a good currying.

Slocum walked to the front and heard voices. He slipped the leather thong off the hammer on his Colt Navy. Gut instinct told him he was walking into a den of rattlers.

"You don't know where your brother is?" demanded a gruff man, almost as tall as Slocum but more heavily built. Big walrus mustaches twitched as he spoke, and a drop of spittle clung to his lip hair. Slocum had never seen the man before—but he knew the man standing behind him.

Federal Marshal Hanssen moved so Slocum got a good look at him. Their eyes locked, and Slocum knew he was in a world of trouble. That glint always showed the utter concentration of a man getting ready to kill.

Slocum's hand flashed for his six-shooter. He cleared leather, cocked, and pointed his Colt before the marshal got his hogleg halfway out of his holster.

"Don't move, Marshal," Slocum ordered. "Tell the rest of your deputies to stand where they are or there's going to be blood shed. And it'll likely be yours."

"Hold on, men," Hanssen said. "This is the other one we want. He's just about as dangerous."

"What are you talking about?" asked Lizbeth, obviously confused. "This is John Slocum. He's my friend."

"And your brother's partner," Hanssen said.

"I told you I don't know where Billy is. You never asked about John."

The deputies were drifting apart, getting ready to throw down on Slocum and catch him in a deadly cross fire. He might gun down their marshal, but they would get him. He couldn't get all six, no matter how he tried.

"What's this all about, Marshal?" Slocum asked.

"We want you and your partner, Slocum. The list of crimes is mounting and getting more horrible by the day."

"I haven't done anything," he lied. Slocum couldn't get that foolish stagecoach robbery out of his mind. He hadn't taken any money. Every dime had been taken by Quince—after he killed three men and two women. That crime had convinced Slocum he and Billy weren't going to continue as partners. Slocum could be a cold, cruel man if the occasion warranted. Billy Quince had shown Slocum what it meant to be soulless. The only times he had seen men as willing to kill for the stark pleasure of it had been during the war. More than one had been like Bloody Bill Anderson and Little Archie and even William Quantrill himself when it came to the sheer excitement of murdering.

Slocum had fought the war for a cause, not some personal vendetta or titillation gained from killing.

"We got quite a list of crimes you and Billy done, Slocum," declared Marshal Hanssen. He started reciting them. Ironically, the only one omitted from the list of crimes was the single one he and Quince *had* done together—the stage holdup.

"I didn't do any of those crimes, Marshal," Slocum said. "If they were done, they were done by Billy Quince. His sister and I have been hunting for him to stop him."

"We heard about her, not you. We want you, Slocum.

You're going to stand trial for a powerful lot of crimes.''

Two of the deputies went for the guns at the same time. Slocum could have killed Hanssen, but knew he would never escape if he did. The muzzle of his six-gun lifted and he fired repeatedly into the adobe brick above them. Two slugs ripped off splinters from a supporting beam. The rest brought down a cascade of blinding dust that gave him the chance of ducking, dodging behind a deputy making for him, and shoving the lawman into the others.

Slocum exploded from the front of the boardinghouse like a stuck pig and ran to his horse. He grabbed the reins of the posse's horses and freed the animals. Then he spooked them. Tired as they were, the horses bolted and ran as he whooped and hollered.

From behind came a hail of bullets. He felt the hot breath of one slug passing near his ear. The bullet ripped through the wide brim of his Stetson, but did not take off the hat. Slocum bent low and galloped off. He had only a few minutes head start before the marshal and his deputies retrieved their horses and came after him.

Slocum considered heading back for the river. He could be in Mexico in only a few minutes, safe from Hanssen and his men. But he also knew they would ride to cut off that exit. Since they expected him to make a break for the Rio Grande and sanctuary in Mexico, Slocum veered away and headed west. He remained in Texas, but could cross the river higher up. This might give him much-needed time to elude the posse.

His horse flagged fast, forcing him to slow to a walk. The heat wore him down, but it worked even more cruelly on his horse. Slocum ought to have dismounted and walked the horse to let it get back its wind, but the need to put as much distance between himself and the federal marshal ate at his gut.

He entered the pass and headed northwest, putting the Franklin Mountains on his right side. The river was only a couple miles off. He figured Hanssen would go due south and wait. Slocum would be across the river before the marshal figured out he had been hornswoggled.

It might be Lizbeth would slow down the lawman's pursuit too.

As he walked his horse, Slocum stewed over the injustice of it all. He was hardly pure as the wind-driven-snow. He had killed and robbed in his day, but none of the crimes Hanssen had charged him with were his. All could be laid at Billy Quince's feet. It was bad enough being caught for a crime he had committed. It was worse being chased down for a passel of them he had not.

Slocum hoped the marshal did not think Lizbeth was hiding her brother and threaten her with jail. He hadn't talked enough with the lawman to know if he was that sort, but considering how vicious her brother had become, Hanssen might do anything to stop Billy Quince. Even put his sister into prison, in the mistaken belief Billy would try to save her.

If anything, Billy might get a thrill out of seeing his own flesh and blood hanged.

Slocum had to dismount when his horse began stumbling. He had pushed the animal to the limit. If he got across the Rio Grande, he would be able to rest and get his horse into shape for the trip into the central highlands. Slocum knew a little village where he would be greeted warmly. Not far from the Barranca del Cobre, it was perfect for him to hide in until Billy Quince was caught or killed.

He stopped when he came to the steep bank of the river. Spring runoff had carved a sheer drop. He looked upriver for a place to get into the muddy riverbed and cross into Mexico. He saw nothing and turned toward the south.

He didn't find a better crossing, but he did see something that sent a cold shiver up his spine. Riders. Riders coming fast.

"Come on," he said, swatting his horse on the rump to get it moving. "We have to cross now."

The horse balked. Slocum grabbed his rifle from the saddle scabbard, abandoned his horse, and jumped the ten feet down into the river bottom. He hit hard and rolled, coming to his feet. His horse whinnied at the mistreatment, providing a sound for the posse to follow. Slocum had hoped the horse would run off and create a moment of diversion.

Instead, the horse brought the lawmen down on his head.

"Give up, Slocum. We're not lettin' you get away!" shouted Marshal Hanssen.

Slocum slogged his way through the thick mud in the center of the river.

"Give up. We're not gonna let you escape. We'll follow you into Mexico if we have to!"

Slocum didn't answer. He waited for the marshal to open fire on him. Exposed as he was, he would be an easy target. The best he could hope for would be to return fire and force the lawmen to take cover, giving him few more minutes to reach the safety of Mexican soil.

But Hanssen didn't open up on him. The lawman kept shouting his empty promises and dire threats if Slocum didn't surrender. Slocum worked at the sucking mud, almost wishing the water was flowing fast so he could swim rather than walk.

"You're gonna swing, Slocum. I won't let you and Quince get away with such vile crimes."

"Wasn't me, Marshal!" Slocum shouted back. "Billy's gone crazy. It's all his doing." Slocum didn't like declaring his former partner was a mad-dog killer, but it was the truth. He wasn't going to be painted with the same brush because of Billy's need to kill any living thing he stumbled across.

Covered in mud, exhausted by the sun and the exertion of crossing the Rio Grande, Slocum worked his way up the steep dirt and gravel bank on the Mexican side of the river.

Safe!

He looked up into the muzzles of three rifles, all held by Marshal Hanssen's deputies. They had crossed the river and gotten in front of him. He had no choice. Arresting him here might not be legal, but who would complain? The *federales*, even if they had been present, could be bought off.

Slocum weighed his choices in a flash. He could fight and die. Or he could surrender. The answer he came to wasn't a pleasant one, but he had no choice. He dropped his rifle and put up his hands.

8

Slocum marched back across the muddy riverbed, hands grabbing for sky. Trailing him were the three deputies. But Slocum saw a faint ray of hope materialize as he worked his way up the steep riverbank on the U.S. side. By the time he got to the top, he saw the El Paso marshal was arguing with Hanssen over whose prisoner Slocum was to be.

"You cain't jist waltz on in here," the El Paso lawman said loudly, "and take *my* prisoner."

"I caught him fair and square." Hanssen motioned to the pair of deputies with him to position themselves to take custody of Slocum. The three behind him shifted their rifles from Slocum's back to the El Paso marshal's badge. Hope surged. If they got to bickering, Slocum might get away.

"You never made your presence known to me, Hanssen. If it hadn't been for my diligent deppity over there with the double-barreled scattergun aimed at your haid, I'd never have knowed you was in town nosin' around my burrow like a hungry hound dog."

"Most of his crimes were in New Mexico Territory. That makes him *my* prisoner," Hanssen insisted. Hanssen stiffened when he saw more of the local marshal's men moving into place, ready for a real fight over Slocum's custody.

"He's mine," the El Paso marshal said truculently. "Daid? You wanna talk about daid men? We got 'em. He kin go to trial here in a few days since we got our very own judge. Judge Magoffin's a fair man."

"He committed crimes in my jurisdiction," Hanssen said obstinately, but Slocum saw the federal marshal was running out of steam. He might have five deputies backing him, but the El Paso marshal had more. The men riding with him might not carry badges pinned on their vests, but they were all armed and apparently looked to the local lawman for their orders. And more came riding up with every passing minute of argument.

"What if we split the reward?" Hanssen began.

"We kin talk this little matter over at our leisure. I think the bar in the Paso del Norte Hotel's a fine place to discuss the matter."

"My whistle does need a bit of wettin'," Hanssen agreed, but Slocum saw the federal marshal wasn't happy giving up his prisoner *or* sharing whatever reward had been put on Slocum and Quince's heads.

"Why don't you boys see our guest on back to the jailhouse?" suggested the El Paso marshal. "Me and my new friend's got things to cuss and discuss."

Laughing, the man rode off. Slocum was left in the middle of a small army of deputies, all wary of each other. If he had a fresh horse he might have capitalized on it, but his horse could barely stumble along in exhaustion. He hoped it would be tended well, because he doubted he would be able to tend it any time soon.

Hanssen shot Slocum a cold look, then trailed after the El Paso marshal. Slocum found himself circled by angry men, all wanting to join their bosses in some saloon to get drunker than lords to celebrate their victory over crime. Once they had Slocum safely in a cell, they could go carousing. Until then, they would as soon plug him as talk to him.

Slocum looked for any chance to escape, but never got

it. Heart heavy and his gut tied into a knot, Slocum dismounted in front of the jail and was escorted in by three deputies. The building looked sturdy, built from brick and rock with mortar in the chinks. The building sat out by itself, lonely and visible from a distance, a few buildings directly across the street from it. Anyone sneaking up on the place from the outside would be seen immediately. A jail break would have to be daring—and probably bloody as hell.

"Got a client for you, Josh," one of the El Paso deputies called to the portly jailer. "He's the one what's been kickin' up dust all over the territory."

"The one riding with Billy Quince?" The jailer eyed Slocum as if he were a bug about to be crushed under a boot heel. "Don't look so tough. You have any trouble with him?"

"He didn't put up even a bit of fuss," the El Paso deputy said, grinning widely. "Hell, them fancy boys from up in Santa Fe didn't have any trouble with him. That ought to tell you he's nowhere near as rowdy as they been sayin'."

"Twenty men dead, five women, and that little boy. I'd say he's powerful mean. Get on into the back, you." The jailer turned a key in a heavy wood door with a thick iron lock, and waited for Slocum to precede him into the dim, cool cell block. Cells on either side held a dozen men, some sleeping, most staring at him as if he had three heads. No one said a word.

They all knew who the new prisoner was. Word traveled fast, especially in a tight community like this one.

He watched for a chance to jump the turnkey, but never got it. The man was wary of such a desperate character, and put Slocum by himself into a cell at the back of the jailhouse.

"Don't want you contaminatin' the others. Most of them are just noisy drunks. Don't want you turnin' them into killers too." The jailer twisted the key in the lock on Slocum's cell door and stepped back. "I might feed you. If I don't forget."

Slocum sat on the narrow cot in the cell and considered his position. He had been in jail before, but never with such a dismal future. He had no friends on the outside to help him break out. He laughed harshly and without humor thinking that the old Billy Quince might try to help. The new one would dance a jig thinking Slocum might die. The only downside for Quince would be that he didn't have a hand in the killing.

And Slocum knew he was not going to be well treated. By the time the other prisoners had finished dinner and he had not seen any food, he knew he was already convicted of the crimes Marshal Hanssen had charged him with.

"It's a crime, not feeding you. At least they let you have water," his lawyer said. The man smelled of too much whiskey and slurred his words slightly, showing he had started early in the morning on his drinking. "How long has it been since they gave you any food?"

"Three days," Slocum said. His belly rumbled, but getting his fill of water from the pitcher on the table in front of him seemed more important. He drank deeply, and would not have gotten any more if his lawyer hadn't demanded it of the bailiff.

"Hits the spot, doesn't it?" asked his lawyer. Slocum almost asked the man what his name was, then stopped. It didn't matter. Coming into the courtroom, Marshal Hanssen looked around and then sat directly behind Slocum.

"You're gonna swing, Slocum, 'less you tell me where your partner is. Got word he killed a buffalo soldier up near Fort Bayard. Shot him in the back of the head."

"It's all Billy Quince's doing," Slocum said, as much to the lawyer as to Marshal Hanssen. "I was helping his sister try to find and stop him. He's gone loco."

"Your hands are clean, huh? Tell it to the jury and see if they believe you. I reckon at least four of them gents have had relatives killed in the past few weeks—by you and Quince.'' Hanssen pointed to the double doors leading into the room.

The jury entered the courtroom, and Slocum knew he was doomed. The twelve men clustered together, pointed at him, and glared. One went so far as to spit in his direction. The bailiff shoved the man toward the jury box and then turned to bellow, ''All stand for the judge.''

Judge Magoffin bustled in, his black robes swirling around him. He mopped at his florid face and said, ''Let's get this over with. The room's hotter 'n the Hell I'm going to send that varmint to.''

Slocum nudged his lawyer, who shook his head.

''Be seated,'' the bailiff said.

The testimony went fast, too fast for Slocum's liking. Marshal Hanssen gave a quick rundown of the crimes Quince had committed, tarring Slocum with each and every one. The El Paso marshal gave a quick testimony about two men and a woman killed down in Ysleta, which was followed by an outburst from two men in the jury box. Slocum didn't have to be told a wife and a sister had been killed—and her memory was represented on the jury by the two men.

''They're going to lynch me,'' Slocum said to his lawyer. The man had asked only a few desultory questions, which Slocum thought did more harm than good. Slocum could have done a better job representing himself.

''There might be extenuating circumstances,'' the man said, drawing out the syllables. He reached into his briefcase and took a quick pull from a bottle of whiskey. Slocum wished he could ask for a drink too. It might kill the pain of having his neck stretched by a rope.

After the last witness, it was over. Slocum's lawyer had no defense and said, ''We throw ourselves on the mercy of the court, Your Honor.'' The lawyer sat heavily, looking pleased with himself.

The judge turned and asked the jury, ''You boys need

any time to think on this or have you decided?''

As one, the men yelled, ''Guilty!''

The foreman went a little further and said, ''Do we string him up or you gonna get someone to do it so we can all watch?''

''No need. We got an executioner on the way up from Austin. He'll be here day after tomorrow. To make this formal, I sentence you to hang by your scrawny neck till you're dead, John Slocum.''

Slocum rose and coldly stared at the judge.

''You got something to say?''

''Do I get a last meal? The marshal hasn't fed me in three days.''

Laughter broke out in the courtroom. The judge gaveled the audience to silence.

''Feed him. Even a dog deserves that much. See you in Hell, Slocum.'' The judge rapped his gavel a last, final time and left, mopping the sweat from his face and stripping off his judge's robes as he went. Slocum was yanked away by the marshal and two deputies.

''We'll appeal!'' the lawyer called. ''This is a miscarriage of justice!''

Marshal Hanssen roughly shoved Slocum toward the side door leading to an alley. ''You deserved better 'n his like,'' he said, referring to the lawyer, ''but even with the best there ever was, you'd still have swung, Slocum. Go to your grave knowin' you done what you could to stop your partner. Tell me where to find Quince.''

''Right now, if I found him you wouldn't have to worry anymore,'' Slocum said. A crowd shouted and threw rotted vegetables and worse at Slocum as the lawmen hustled him back to the jailhouse.

''You better bring in a couple extra guards,'' Hanssen told the El Paso marshal. ''You want my boys to help out? We ain't goin' back to Santa Fe till he's stretched and buried.''

"No need. We've kept tougher ones than him in this jail."

"I don't guess it matters much if the crowd lynches him," Hanssen said. "But the judge might think poorly of it if he went to the expense of sendin' for the official state's executioner. And the executioner might not like it havin' to come all this way for nothin'." With that Hanssen left.

Slocum saw the local marshal wasn't moved by the idea that a lynch mob might take his prisoner. He saw Slocum was secure in the back cell, then turned to the jailer and said, "I'm going to find me some lunch. Maybe down at the Oriental Saloon. Heard tell they're puttin' out a special spread in honor of the verdict."

"Save me some, Marshal," the jailer said.

Slocum sank to the cot and looked around the cell. For three days he had hunted for a way out. There didn't seem to be anything he could do to get through the steel bars and straps circling the cage. The window was high and small, hardly large enough for him to wiggle through if there hadn't been strong bars blocking his way outside. Once outside, Slocum remembered the solitary nature of the jail-house. He needed a horse and a lot of luck ever to get away from the two marshals and an outraged El Paso population.

The only way out was through the securely locked door. And he wasn't likely to pass through again until they took him out in shackles to the public hanging.

Slocum went to sleep that night listening to the pounding of hammers driving nails into wood supports in his gallows.

9

"No guilty man ever goes to the gallows," opined the man in the cell next to Slocum's. " 'Cept in your case, Slocum. You're guilty as bloody hell!"

Slocum lay back, trying not to respond to the taunts. The other prisoners took turns trying to rile him. He kept his mind focused on the problem of getting free. The only way he could possibly clear himself was getting Billy Quince to confess. Slocum knew that wasn't likely to happen before the hanging.

That meant he had to escape from the El Paso jail. But how? This cell had been built to hold the strongest, most determined prisoner. The only chance he saw came in jumping the jailer when he delivered dinner. *His last meal.* The three words rattled in his head, over and over until he wanted to scream.

His last meal, unless he jumped the jailer, got past any guards in the outer jail, and stole a horse and . . .

There were too many "ands" for him to believe he had much of a chance. That didn't stop him from trying, though. If he got lucky, the jailer or a guard might shoot him. Better to die cleanly from a bullet in the gut than to have his neck broken when he fell with a knotted rope around his throat.

"Here it is, Slocum," called the jailer. The man dropped

a small, dirty tin plate to the floor and cautiously pushed it toward the cell door with the toe of his boot. Slocum had no chance to grab the man to force him to give up the cell keys. Even if he had managed to grab him, Slocum saw the jailer had wisely left the keys back in the office, far from grasping fingers.

He stared at the battered tin plate and wondered if Hell could be any worse than El Paso. The jailer laughed viciously, as if he could read his thoughts.

"What's wrong, Slocum? Don't like beans? I put lots of salt on 'em, just for you!" The man clutched his bulging gut and left, laughing uproariously. Slocum saw he didn't get even a small cup of water to go with the beans. Worse than salt, he saw green slivers of jalapeño floating among the greasy beans. If he choked down this slop, he would end up with a mouth drier than the Chihuahua Desert south of town.

"You figurin' Billy Quince is gonna come to spring you, Slocum?" called another prisoner.

"I'm figuring he will slit your worthless throat in the middle of the night," Slocum said, angry now. This threat shut the others up. They sank to their bunks. Before too much longer, snores were the only mocking sounds reaching him.

He wasn't going to get a chance to jump the jailer or steal the keys to the cell. He wasn't getting to eat. And his mouth had turned to gummy cotton from lack of water. They not only intended to hang him, they were torturing him.

"Damn your eyes, Billy," he muttered. Slocum made another circuit of the small cell, hunting for any weakness in the bars he might have missed before. The search turned up nothing new. Slocum flopped back onto the cot to wait for sunup and his execution.

Try as he might, Slocum couldn't stop thinking what he would do to Quince when he caught up with him. The idea was absurd. He was going to swing in a few hours and would never get the chance. But Billy Quince had gotten him into this fix, and all Slocum could do was think of creative ways of getting back at him.

The Apaches had nothing on John Slocum and his schemes for revenge.

He heard a tiny clinking sound that brought him up. He moved to the door when he saw a dim figure flitting like a ghost through the cell block, going from prisoner to prisoner. Whatever the small figure hunted for was not found until it stopped in front of his cell.

Slocum's eyes went wide. This was the last person in the world he had expected to see. And she was opening his cell door.

"Hurry, unless you wish to dangle by your neck," the Rio Kid's widow whispered.

"Why are you—?" He got no farther. She thrust a gun at him. He took the six-shooter and hefted it. His Colt Navy felt good in his grip again.

She motioned, and they retraced the path to the door. Slocum pushed past her and glanced out, ready to shoot it out with the marshal's deputies and the jailer. The jailer slept quietly, head on folded arms at the desk. Two guards were slumped in wooden chairs, both snoring loudly. No one would notice them leaving.

"What'd you do?"

"Whiskey," she said. Then the woman grinned to show rows of perfect white teeth. "It held the knockout drug."

"Chloral hydrate," he said. "Why are you risking your neck to save me?"

She put a finger to her lips. She had heard what Slocum hadn't. Footsteps. He cocked his six-gun and aimed it directly at the door. There was no way he'd ever be put back in the cell to be executed. Better to shoot it out here and now.

The door opened a fraction. Whoever was outside hesitated before pushing on into the marshal's office. Slocum's heart hammered in his chest. Was this Marshal Hanssen with a dozen deputies? A lynch mob come to string him up now? The door opened wide enough for Slocum to see the face. He heaved a deep sigh and lowered the six-shooter.

"Hurry up, you two," Lizbeth Quince said. "I've got the horses. You need to get back across the river, Consuela."

"Consuela?" Slocum looked at the Rio Kid's widow. She nodded. He had never known her name. "Thank you, Consuela," he said.

"I have pulled your fat from the fire. No more. And you will repay me, no questions asked."

"All right. We can talk this over when we get away."

"We will meet in a day. In Mesilla. She knows where." With that, Consuela vanished into the night. Slocum stood beside Lizbeth, staring into her bright blue eyes. He wanted to kiss her.

She grabbed his arm and dragged him along. "No time," she said. "I've got four horses so we can make a quick getaway."

"How'd you think of that?" he asked.

"Why, I read all the penny dreadfuls. I know how you do things out on the frontier. Mr. Ned Buntline has—"

"Come on," Slocum said. He didn't care how she had thought to bring spare horses for them. She had done the right thing to make escape easier. He checked the cinches to be sure they were tight. Whoever had saddled the horses knew his business. "Where's this Mesilla?"

"To the north, on the west side of the Franklin Mountains," she said. "We'll meet Consuela there later."

"She won't turn us in for the reward?" Slocum asked, mounting.

"Why would she help me get you out, then do something like that?"

Slocum had plenty of time to think on such double crosses. The answer came easily.

"I wasn't worth two hoots and a holler to anybody in

jail. With me escaping, the reward might be put back on my head. Almost definitely will. She can turn me in to Marshal Hanssen and get enough money to live on for a long, long time.''

''I went to her for help,'' Lizbeth said. They trotted through the dark, empty streets, moving west and then curving toward the north when they got through the pass. This was the route he had taken trying to escape before. He considered crossing the river again and going into the heart of Mexico where no U.S. lawman would ever find him. But he owed Lizbeth the chance to explain her plan.

She had done a sight better than he had so far arranging for him to get free.

''Ahead,'' he said. Outside a saloon he saw a small group of bluecoats. He didn't want the cavalry on his heels. He took a side street to get around the gin mill, then cut back and urged his horse to more speed. He wanted to ride it until it was half dead, then switch to the other horse, but he kept the pace below a gallop. Get as much out of this one before switching, he told himself. Distance mattered. If the law didn't know what direction he headed, every minute he rode was that much more of a guarantee he would get away scot-free.

They soon made it out into range land. He heard cattle lowing in the distance, and saw shadowy movement of coyotes and other predators beginning to stir. It wasn't long until sunrise. Slocum reached up and ran his hand around his neck. It felt good the way it was.

''Mesilla is a stagecoach way station,'' Lizbeth said.

''To Tombstone and Tucson.'' He remembered now. ''Those seem like good places to head. Then we can reach the coast and figure where to go from there.''

''We need to hole up for a day or two, John,'' she said. ''It's part of my payment for getting you out of jail.''

''I owe you my life,'' he said, remembering the last time he had said that to someone. It had been to Lizbeth's brother. Paddy Patterson had almost blown off Slocum's head and Billy had shot the rustler, saving Slocum from an early grave.

"Then you will listen to what Consuela and I have to say, when she arrives."

"We have a definite place to go or do we just crawl into a cave somewhere?" He looked at the rugged Organ Mountains ahead. To his right were the taller Franklins, now outlined with the light of a new day. That sight made him put his heels to his horse and get it moving a tad faster. The horse tired quickly now. Slocum switched to the other, giving his first mount the chance to rest up without a rider.

As he rode, he wished the Rio Grande carried more water than it did. Finding a few muddy spots with standing water provided most of their water—and their horses'—as they crossed the summer-parched countryside strewn with prickly pear cactus and ocotillo. The heat hammered at them savagely and sucked the precious moisture from their bodies fast. The two canteens of water Lizbeth had brought were quickly exhausted, but Slocum refused to slow the pace and hunt for water along the road. Most travelers started north with ample supplies. He couldn't fault Lizbeth for not bringing more; how was she to know they would go through so much water so quickly?

"John, I'm getting a mite dizzy," Lizbeth said after they had ridden for another hour. Any sane person would have sought shade and waited until the hottest part of the day passed. He was sane, but he wasn't stupid. Marshal Hanssen would be after him all too soon.

"There's a barrel cactus," he said. He dropped to the ground and cut out a plug of juicy, bitter pulp. "Suck on it until the sap is gone." He took one for himself. It tasted bad, but it would keep them alive for another few miles. That was the way he came to think about it. Another mile, another few yards, a foot.

Just one more. To get away.

He wished he had water for the horses more than for

himself. If the horses flagged, the law would recapture him in the wink of an eye.

He and Lizbeth crossed the fifty miles to Mesilla by nightfall, and found a spot to camp in a dry arroyo a half mile away from the edge of town. This was still too close to civilization for Slocum's liking, what with marshals and sheriffs and other lawmen poking about all the time, but he felt safer here than trying to find a place to camp in the mountains now that it was dark.

"You thought of everything," Slocum said, poking through the saddlebags and finding enough food to last him on the trail for weeks. He took out a can of beans and another of peaches. It wasn't a Delmonico steak, but it seemed like the finest victuals he had ever tasted after his stint in the El Paso jail.

Lizbeth built a small fire in the center of the arroyo and heated the beans while Slocum went to find water. It took him longer to do that than it did for her to fix their simple supper. She tried to talk to him, but he was ravenous and devoured the food, following it with as much water as he could swallow without bloating.

"They starved me in jail," he explained. "No water, or not much, either."

"They are animals."

"I can't say I was pleased with the treatment," Slocum said, "but I can understand why they were all willing to do it. They're trying to get even for some pretty awful crimes committed against their friends and families. The way I see it, I have to bring in Billy so he can confess what all he has done and get me off the hook—or at least away from the gallows."

Even as he spoke, Slocum knew he wasn't likely to succeed. Billy Quince was on a killing spree. He might be dead already. If he wasn't, Slocum had almost no chance of finding him before the law. Even if he did, Slocum doubted he could force Quince to come clean and confess he had murdered all those people on his own.

"We can talk about Billy when Consuela gets here tomorrow," Lizbeth said. "Right now, I just want to forget about . . . everything." She moved her bedroll closer to his and sat, her arms around him. Her warmth contrasted with the cold desert wind whipping through the scrub brush and mesquite trees now. He held her, and it felt natural, good, as if he had always been intended to be like this.

They lay back, their arms still circling each other's bodies. Slocum wasn't sure exactly who started and who followed. It might have been Lizbeth, or he could have done it. A button came free. Then another and another. A rustle of cloth, the lifting of a skirt. The tug on his jeans. His hardness jutting out. A feminine hand circling it and stroking up and down it until intense need filled him.

They kissed. Their lips crushed together. Then Lizbeth's lips parted slightly. Her tongue slipped free and teased and tormented his. They danced about, played hide and seek, going from mouth to mouth, and both of them were past the point of stopping.

His hands moved down the front of her unfastened blouse. He found the smooth, sleek mounds of her breasts. He pressed them until they were almost flat. The hard nubbins at the crests began to throb with every beat of Lizbeth's heart. It pulsed as fast as his own.

He pulled his mouth away from hers and tasted the salty tang of her nipples, licking and sucking and turning her into a moaning creature intent only on pleasure.

"Yes, John, oh, so good, so very nice. But I want more."

So did he, but he wasn't going to rush this. He had gobbled supper. He wanted to savor this lovemaking.

He worked down lower, his lips and tongue touching and kissing as he went into the crinkly bush nestled between her legs. She lifted her knees and spread her legs wide as he rooted about. His tongue flashed out and touched her here and there, causing Lizbeth's hips to lift off the ground. She ground herself into his face.

But it wasn't enough for either of them. Slocum felt the

tension mount in his loins until he wanted to scream. He ached for what she had to offer. Rolling onto her, he looked down into her bright blue eyes. Lizbeth's dark hair was spread out above her like a fan made of raven's feathers. Never had he seen a woman so lovely and so needy for what he had to give.

She wiggled about to position herself precisely, then reached down and caught at his hardness again. She pulled insistently on his manhood until the tip brushed across the furry triangle where he had so recently licked and kissed.

They both gasped when he shoved forward. He sank all the way into her center. Her legs curled around his waist and her heels locked behind his back, holding him firmly in place. As if he wanted to go anywhere else. He rotated his hips about in a stirring motion that drove both their desires to the limits. Then he backed off.

He ground his body into hers until the world went away in a bedazzling whirl of emotion. All that remained was Lizbeth and his desires and how he could give them both pleasure. He began moving in the age-old rhythm of a man loving a woman. He made it only a few strokes before she lifted off the ground again, this time crushing herself into his groin and twisting her hips around.

Lizbeth gave as good as she got.

Slocum spilled his seed and Lizbeth cried out in ecstasy and they sank into a muzzy afterglow that covered them both for some time. When the cold wind began to nibble at his exposed flesh, Slocum pulled the blanket over them both and returned to sample more of Lizbeth's tempting bodily treats.

Sunrise came and found them both sleeping, but Slocum slowly became aware of a presence nearby. Without waking Lizbeth, he stirred a little, got his six-shooter, and rolled onto his back, feigning sleep. He carefully opened his lids to let in a bit of sunlight, and saw someone bending over their saddlebags. He pushed aside the blanket and aimed his Colt Navy at the intruder.

Without bothering to turn around, Consuela asked, ''Do you not have any coffee? I will fix it for you while you two get dressed.''

Slocum lowered the hammer on his six-gun. He knew the time had come to learn the price for Consuela's help breaking him out of the jail—and saving him from the gallows.

10

"How did you find us?" Slocum asked. He was worried that if Consuela had no difficulty tracking them down, Marshal Hanssen wouldn't either. He figured the federal marshal was a determined man, and probably a good one on the trail.

"I told her where to camp. You are not far away from there. This is better. Nearer the water," Consuela said. She poured water into a cup and drank it. "Not good water, though. Bitter."

Slocum waited for Consuela to turn so he could get on his pants. When she didn't move or avert her eyes, he decided the hell with it and dressed. The woman sat impassively as she sipped her water. Only when he finished tugging on his boots did Lizbeth stir.

"Umm, John, where are you?" Lizbeth reached out to find him. The blanket slid from her shoulder and showed she was naked. Slocum reckoned it didn't much matter to the Rio Kid's widow. She had lived the life of a gunfighter's woman, and must have seen much that was both illegal and immoral.

"Get dressed," Slocum said. "We got company." So as not to startle her, he hastily added, "It's your partner in crime. Consuela."

Lizbeth sat up. Her eyes were still blurry from sleep. Then they fixed on Consuela. A smile lit up Lizbeth's face.

"You made it!" The dark-haired woman quickly dressed. Again Consuela sat impassively, watching, drinking her bitter water, saying and doing nothing more until Lizbeth was decent.

"I want to thank you both for what you've done," Slocum said. Memory of being in the El Paso jail and nearly having his neck stretched would linger for too many years to come.

This finally broke Consuela's stolid expression. She laughed and pointed to Lizbeth. "You have already thanked her, I see. Will you thank me in this way too?"

"You're not going to—" Lizbeth began, far too possessively for Slocum's liking.

"No, no, I want nothing to do with this one," Consuela said. "To be with him is to ride the tornado, I think. Just like my dearly departed *novio*."

"You're right, Consuela! But we didn't get John out of that horrible jail—spring him, I think the term is—just for him to ride off. Do you agree you owe us, John?"

Slocum nodded, wondering where this was heading. He thought he knew, and it didn't please him. He had already come to a conclusion about what to do with the rest of his life. Or at least the next few months. What Lizbeth and Consuela were going to ask wasn't in the cards.

"The spurs, John. We want you to find Billy and . . ."

". . . and destroy the spurs," Consuela finished. "You *must* destroy the cursed spurs. They were fashioned for a *vaquero*, not a gunman."

"How am I supposed to do this?" Slocum asked.

"Melt them in a forge," suggested Consuela.

"Bury them somewhere in the desert where nobody will ever find them," Lizbeth said. "But take them off Billy and destroy them. You owe us your life. You can destroy the spurs for us to keep anyone else's life from being ruined."

"That's not what I meant," Slocum said, suddenly tired, as if the weight of the world sank fully on his shoulders. "How do I avoid the lawmen hunting me *and* find Billy? Finding him will be hard enough, but doing it with a posse on my trail makes it almost impossible." Slocum held up his hand to stop the women from arguing the point with him. "There's something else you haven't thought about. With so much reward money riding on Billy's head, bounty hunters from all over the West will be flocking here to come after him. What if one of them gets to Billy first, and *he* takes the spurs?"

"Then you must hunt down this bounty hunter and destroy the spurs," Consuela insisted. "I do not care for this man who was your partner, her brother. I want only to remove forever from the earth what destroyed my husband. Get rid of the spurs!"

Slocum knew he was signing his own death warrant. Getting out of the territory was the smartest thing he could do right now. Putting as much distance as possible between him and El Paso—and the federal marshal from Santa Fe— was the only way to stay alive. He had a death sentence waiting for him if any lawman caught him.

And that might be the easy part, riding around the Southwest with the law breathing down his neck. How could he find Quince? Billy had shown his willingness to travel long distances, killing as he went to remove witnesses. By the time Slocum could learn of a new mass killing, Quince might be a hundred miles away—in any direction.

He was taking on an impossible job.

"All right," he said. His sense of honor was too strong to even consider agreeing and then heading for the Dakotas as he had planned. Slocum would do his best to destroy the spurs. If he avoided the executioner's noose along the way, all the better.

"Who wants to live forever?" asked Consuela. She didn't even smile when she said it. With a quick tilt of the cup, she finished the water. "I will expect you to do as you have promised."

"He will," Lizbeth said. "I have full faith in him."

That statement was another nail in his coffin, as far as Slocum was concerned. Disappointing Lizbeth Quince would be as bad as going back on his word.

"*Bueno,*" Consuela said. She tossed the cup aside, stood, and walked off without so much as a backward glance. Slocum figured she must have tethered her horse some distance away, because he never heard her ride off.

"How are we going to find Billy?" asked Lizbeth, anxious now to hear all the details he had not worked out for himself. "Can we find him at the campsite where you—"

"You're not coming with me," Slocum said.

"But John, I can help. Haven't I got you out of jail? I can talk to Billy. You said yourself he might shoot you on sight. He won't do that to me."

Slocum had had plenty of time to think about Billy Quince while he wasted away in the El Paso jail. He didn't bother telling Lizbeth what he thought her precious brother might do to her if she happened across him alone. He took a deep breath, collected his thoughts, and only then did he tell her what he had to.

"If the marshal catches you with me, you might end up in jail. Go on back to El Paso and wait where I can find you. Miss Peabody's boardinghouse, if she hasn't thrown you out already. But I have to hunt down your brother alone. It's the only way."

He saw her thinking on it. She bit her lower lip and forced back tears. Then she wiped away the tiny trails that left muddy tracks like claw marks in the dust on her cheeks. Lizbeth forced a slight smile and held out her arms to him.

Silently, he went to her and they made love. Then he rode off, Lizbeth crying softly as he went.

Slocum couldn't figure out who was on his trail. He had doubled back twice hoping to catch sight of his tracker, and hadn't succeeded. It might be his nerves, he knew, but he didn't think so. His sixth sense had kept him alive for a lot of years, and it told him now that someone dogged his steps, whether he saw him or not.

Sitting atop a rock in the foothills of the Florida Mountains, he studied the severe countryside he had just crossed. Hoping for a hint of swirling dust, the flash of sunlight off an exposed hunk of metal, some clue to who followed him, Slocum sat and watched patiently as he ate a can of beans. He had two left in his saddlebags, so he savored this one as much as he could.

From now on he would have to take time to hunt food. The few rabbits he had seen poking long-eared heads from their burrows were scrawny and wary. The weather had been particularly hot this year, and no rain had fallen in months. It might be the end of July before the rains came, almost a month off. Eating lizards was a lousy way to keep alive, but Slocum would do it if he had to.

Watching for a bushwhacker at every turn was no better a way to go through life, yet Slocum did it. He had been on Quince's trail for ten days now, and felt no closer to running him down. Slocum wished he could say the same about whoever chased *him*. Hot breath on the back of his neck made him shudder in dread.

His beans done, he tossed the airtight as far as he could to his left. Let the tracker find it and think Slocum had taken a game trail to the top of the ridge. Slocum stuck to the lower elevations, seeking water and places where Billy Quince might have camped. He and Quince had come through here what seemed a lifetime ago, but Slocum doubted the outlaw would come back. There wasn't anyone nearby to kill.

He doubted Quince would come here, but he had to look. He had no other place to start.

The burning hot sun slid down into the heat shimmer of the New Mexican desert, and the sky turned bright red and faint orange and dozens of colors in between that Slocum couldn't put a name to. Amid the spectacle he saw he had not been imagining that he had company on this trail.

A faint cloud of dust rose as the rider trailing him struggled up a dry arroyo bank. The dust settled fast, and the man made his way to a rocky patch to hold down evidence of his tracking. Slocum admired the man's skill even as he dreaded confronting whoever it was.

If it had been Marshal Hanssen's posse, he would have felt better. A solitary rider—and one dedicated to his task like this one—meant a bounty hunter was after him. The man wasn't likely to have his money cut off because the good folks back in Washington refused to pay any more for a posse, or because a deputy had to go home because he got the runs. A bounty hunter went begging unless he brought in his quarry.

John Slocum, prey for a bounty hunter.

What to do next was a poser for Slocum. He couldn't keep dodging a man this good at tracking. He had already tried most of the tricks he had learned over the years, and none had worked. If he bushwhacked the bounty hunter, that might bring down a raft of trouble on his head he didn't want. Hanssen was out there somewhere. The marshal might have followed a lead going in some other direction, Slocum knew, but with the way his luck had been running, he doubted it. If he wanted to stay alive he had to assume those hunting him were right on his heels.

Like this man.

Slocum licked his dried lips, hankered for some whiskey, then figured the best way he could deal with the situation was to put the man on foot. Stealing a horse in this desert might be a death sentence, but Slocum felt better about it than he did about simply shooting the man in the back. That was Billy Quince's way, not his.

Slocum slid down the rock and landed on his feet. He considered how hard it would be for the man to find him, then laid his trap carefully. Slocum let his horse leave a pile of manure, then led the dun-colored horse away, know-

ing the bounty hunter would find the spoor. Slocum
mounted, rode in a wide circle, and came up from behind.

It took him the better part of an hour, but his patience
paid off. The bounty hunter had dismounted, taken his rifle,
and stalked Slocum on foot. Slocum rode up to the man's
horse, tethered to a mesquite tree laden with bean pods.
The horse nibbled at the tasty beans amid the thorny
branches, and hardly noticed when Slocum approached.

He reached over, used his knife, and cut the cinch on the
saddle. The horse let out a contented whinny at the lightened load. Then Slocum tugged the reins free of the thorny
tree and led the horse away. At first, the horse didn't want
to go along, and put up a little fuss that worried Slocum.
Then he saw the horse's flanks. The bounty hunter was not
a compassionate rider. Barely healed weals showed where
he had whipped and spurred his horse to greater speed. In
this desert, in the summer heat, he had pushed the horse to
its limits.

"Old girl," he said to the mare, "you've just got yourself a kinder owner." Horse stealing wasn't a crime that
set well with him. It might doom the bounty hunter to a
slow death, but seeing the horse's condition made the theft
a mite easier for Slocum to do.

"Hey, stop! Thief! Damned horse thief!" came the loud,
angry cry. Slocum urged his horse to greater speed and
clung to the mare's reins. A rifle bullet ripped through the
air over his head. He hunkered down and kept riding.

A mile to the north he slowed. Two miles and he let the
horses walk. Three and he switched, riding bareback on the
mare while his horse rested from the escape. Slocum might
have been content to take a break except he had seen
bounty hunters who seemed more than human in their en-
durance. Years back many were mountain men who no
longer hunted beaver and other fur animals.

Slocum wasn't going to press his luck with this fellow.
The best tactic he could use was getting as far away as
possible and not trying to match wits and skill. He had seen

how the bounty hunter was good at tracking and hiding his own trail.

Throughout the rest of the day, Slocum kept on the move, not fast, but never stopping except to swap horses and partake of the all-too-infrequent watering holes along the path leading into the mountains. He ached, and he knew his horses were nearing the end of their strength by the time he came across the trail.

The trail.

Slocum dropped to the ground and spent fifteen minutes circling the area to be sure he had what he thought. He pushed his hat back and wiped his forehead. A faint dry puff of wind cooled him, but his heart beat faster.

A posse had passed this way within the last twenty-four hours. From what he could tell, at least ten men rode along this trail. He reckoned it was Marshal Hanssen's posse since the El Paso marshal wasn't likely to whip up enough passion on his own to track down Slocum—and Billy Quince. But parallel to trail left by the posse Slocum saw a solitary rider's spoor. Not much, but enough.

It might be Quince or it might be a scout for the posse. There was no way he could tell, other than that the posse headed deeper into the Florida Mountains, where he had thought to find Billy Quince. Things the man had said told Slocum Quince was familiar with this terrain. Before they had thrown together, Quince had done a fair amount of hunting in these hills, or so he had claimed.

Slocum saw no reason to disbelieve Quince—then. Now he wasn't sure what to believe. Follow the posse and run up on them by accident, only to find the marshal had no idea where Billy Quince was? Or keep hunting the killer on his own, hoping the posse flushed Billy so he ran right into Slocum's open arms?

Or something else? Slocum was tossed on the horns of this dilemma. Quince was a slippery customer, but the man wasn't really what Slocum sought so diligently. He had promised both the Rio Kid's widow and Quince's sister he would get the spurs and destroy them. Slocum snorted in disgust. He didn't hold that the spurs were a problem. The men wearing them were the problem. If the Rio Kid or Quince went kill-crazy, it had nothing to do with what clanked at their heels. It had everything to do with what went on under their Stetsons.

Sunstroke or simply loco, Slocum didn't know. It didn't matter either. What meant more was what those men did and the men—and women and children—they left dead in their wake.

He could follow, but he decided to avoid the posse. Billy Quince would likely play with the marshal and then try to slip away. That was the best time for Slocum to find him, when Quince was feeling full of himself because he had hoodwinked the law one more time.

Slocum stretched tired muscles and saw that the horses, in spite of each enduring his weight for only half the day, were likewise tuckered out from the travel through the desert heat. He found a secure place among the rocks for his bivouac, debated a cooking fire, and finally chose to keep a cold camp. The horses had some scrubby grass to crop, and he had one of his remaining cans of beans. Water was scarce, but he could find more after he got back on the trail in the morning by following game along faint dusty trails, not so much to hunt for breakfast as for water that kept the animals alive in this rocky hell.

Content that he had chosen the best course for finding Billy and avoiding Hanssen's posse, Slocum lay back against his saddle, head propped up. He cradled his rifle in the crook of his arm and nodded off an hour after the sun had vanished in the west. How long he slept Slocum was not sure.

He awoke to the sound of someone moving in the rocks above him. He swung around, rifle leveled, when he heard the unmistakable metallic click of a six-shooter cocking.

The bullet aimed at him tore past his head before he could get off his own shot.

11

Slocum jerked away involuntarily as the slug ripped a hole in the brim of his hat. His answering shot missed the bounty hunter by a country mile as Slocum tried to juggle between the necessary acts of dodging and firing. Although he missed, the rifle shot boomed deep and deadly enough to force the bounty hunter to cover, giving Slocum a brief respite. He spun and dove for cover, hoping the man in the rocks above him wouldn't have a good shot at him.

Truth was, Slocum wasn't exactly sure where the other man hid. The crunch of rock, the cocking of his six-shooter, those were the warnings he'd had. Not actual sight of the man. A dim, dark shape looming above had given him a hint where the bounty hunter might be, but he wasn't certain. Especially now.

Slocum wiggled like a snake through the rocks, wondering where his best chance for survival lay. He hadn't seen the man, but figured it had to be the bounty hunter whose horse he had stolen so many hours ago. The man had followed on foot through the hot sun, along the desert and rocky path into the mountainous foothills. Afoot. He had followed on foot and had caught up with Slocum before midnight.

This was one tough hombre. Slocum felt a moment of

regret having to shoot the bounty hunter, but there seemed no other way to get free. Stealing the man's horse had signed his own death warrant, should the bounty hunter get him squarely in his gunsights. Any reward offered for him would only be icing on the cake for the bounty hunter.

"Give up, Slocum," came a gravelly voice. "I don't mean you no harm."

Slocum wondered how stupid the man thought he was. A noose waited for him later if he didn't take a bullet in the gut now. He either rode away free or he died. Those were the only choices facing John Slocum.

He got his feet under him and peered over the top of a boulder. Slight movement where he suspected the bounty hunter to be almost lured him into shooting. The foot-long muzzle flash would give away his position. It wouldn't matter if he ended the bounty hunter's life with the shot. It might mean *his* life if the bounty hunter was suckering him out of hiding.

Slocum watched the shadows moving erratically, and then realized he *was* being suckered. The movement he had spotted was caused by the bounty hunter holding up his coat on a long stick. Slocum followed the stick back to another, denser shadow. He squeezed off a round, and was rewarded by a loud yelp. Slocum cursed. The shot had only winged the bounty hunter. Considering how tough the man had proven himself to be—and how tenacious—this was like kicking a cornered cougar.

Slocum ducked back, then made his way to his left as fast as he could, hoping to circle the bounty hunter and get the drop on him from behind. Slocum had gotten halfway to the spot where he figured he could carry out his plan when a fusillade of slugs tore away at him. Falling flat on his belly, he let the bounty hunter empty his six-shooter. He tried to remember how many rounds had come his way, and couldn't.

He took a desperate gamble and scrambled up, hoping to catch the man as he reloaded.

It almost cost Slocum his life. Riding with Quantrill's Raiders ought to have taught him about dangerous men. Every one of Quantrill's guerrillas carried eight or ten pistols, giving them the firepower of a company three times their size. Slocum had been foolish thinking the bounty hunter carried only a single six-shooter.

The second gun blazed away at him. Slocum felt sharp pain in his leg as a slug tore away his flesh. He fell forward, triggering a round in the direction of the bounty hunter. He missed, and did nothing to keep the bounty hunter from firing again at him. Slocum fell heavily and tried to get up. His leg gave way under him. He slumped back, side pressed against a sharp rock. He didn't move.

"Where'd you go, you miserable horse-thievin' varmint?" growled the bounty hunter. Slocum heard the man blundering around. The soft clicking of cartridges slipping into the cylinders of his six-shooters warned Slocum of the folly of a frontal attack again. He lay still, wondering if the bounty hunter would come after him or play a waiting game.

Slocum pressed a hand against the wound on his leg, sizing up the crease and deciding it hurt more than anything else. Already the wound had caked over and the numbness from the initial shock of impact had faded. He could walk. He could even run.

If he had to.

"I don't let nobody steal *my* horse," the bounty hunter said. "No, sir, nobody steals Big Mike O'Leary's horse."

Slocum knew the man hoped to spook him. Slocum had never heard of the bounty hunter, but that didn't matter. He wanted Slocum to think he was big and tough, but Slocum wondered just how true that was.

Moving as quietly as he could, Slocum slipped away, retracing his path to this spot. He moved quieter than a shadow, and soon found himself near his camp again. A bullet hole in his saddle told how close he had come to having his head blown off earlier. A quick step and a jump got him into the rocks directly under where Big Mike O'Leary had first attacked. Slocum scrambled up and found the exact spot where the bounty hunter had kicked out the spent brass and reloaded.

How much ammo do you have? Slocum silently wondered of the bounty hunter. He had taken the man's horse and saddlebags, not checking to see what was in them. Big Mike might have only a pocketful of ammunition with him, enough for his purposes as he dropped to study a trail. There hadn't been any good reason for the man to expect a big fight when he'd left his horse to be stolen.

Slocum did what he could to follow the bounty hunter through the darkness, listening hard. Big Mike was a giant of a man, but he moved with a surprisingly soft step. After so many miles trudging through the desert, that he could walk at all was amazing. Slocum knew he faced a worthy opponent.

As the thought crossed his mind that he might be better off hightailing it, he heard a tiny click of rock against rock. He spun, rifle ready to fire. A meaty hand batted it from his grip. Slocum felt himself caught up by powerful arms that threatened to crush the life from him as they tightened around his chest.

"Gotcha, ya little son of a bitch. I was gonna kill ya, but I want to see ya suffer first."

The world spun around Slocum's head and his vision began blurring as the mountain of a man punished him. His rifle had fallen from his grip, and his arms were pinned under the steely bands of the bounty hunter's forearms.

"I wanted Quince 'fore he got hisself kilt, but you got a powerful big bounty on yer head. Don't know why. You're almost too easy to run to earth."

Slocum strained and gained a fraction of an inch of space—for an instant. Then the weight of Big Mike's grip closed in on him again.

"Let me go," Slocum gasped out.

"Not till I done ya good for what ya—" Big Mike's

eyes went wide when the Colt Navy discharged into his belly. For a ghastly second, Slocum thought that was all the response he was going to get from the bounty hunter. Then the grip eased and Big Mike stumbled back, sitting down hard on a rock and clutching his abdomen.

He pressed his fingers into the tiny .36-caliber hole, then looked up at Slocum in disbelief.

"You shot me. You kilt me!"

Slocum gasped for breath. He had dropped his six-shooter after firing it. His arms had turned to lead from the punishment meted out by the bounty hunter. If he had tried to fire a second round, he would have failed. As it was, his first shot had been lucky and must have cut through vital organs inside the bounty hunter. Otherwise, Big Mike would have squeezed until Slocum was crushed flat.

"I coulda got a heap of money for ya, but it's Quince I wanted, 'fore, 'fore he . . ."

"Before he what?" demanded Slocum. His strength came back slowly, but he was strong enough to pick up his trusty six-gun. Even with Big Mike slowly yielding to death's cold embrace, Slocum kept the pistol aimed squarely at the bounty hunter's torso. He respected him and his determination that much.

"I—" Big Mike gasped and spat blood. Pink froth came to his lips. Slocum had not only blasted through the man's intestines, but had also punctured a lung.

"You wanted to stop Quince's massacre?"

"Now, not that. Hell, Slocum, folks die all the time." Big Mike spat again and looked at him. His eyes were glazing over as his sight faded. "I wanted him 'fore he got hisself kilt. What a fool. Nobody goes against Hardin and lives. Nobody, not even Billy Quince."

"What are you talking about?"

Big Mike slid down the rock, mouth open to reply, but no words came out. He was dead.

"What *were* you talking about?" Slocum corrected himself. It made no sense. Quince and Hardin? John Wesley

Hardin? What did he have to do with Billy Quince? Slocum searched the dead bounty hunter's body and found wads of wanted posters. If Big Mike had returned even a small fraction of the men pictured he would have been rich.

But John Wesley Hardin? Slocum shook his head. He sat and waited until his weakness passed. He got to his feet, determined to warn Lizbeth of her brother's intent to call out Hardin. That was the only sense Slocum could make of the bounty hunter's last words. Billy Quince wanted another notch for his six-shooter's handle—one for the deadliest, orneriest, most cold-blooded killer who ever rode the range.

Loco or not, spurs or not, Quince could never take Hardin. Too many dead men had thought they were faster. Some had thought they were sneakier, trying to gun down Hardin from ambush. Another had burned down a hotel the gunfighter had slept in. Hardin was always a step ahead, a shade faster, far more accurate with his lethal six-gun.

And he had no conscience about killing. Hardin might not even notice when Billy Quince died.

"Why'd I get involved in this?" grumbled Slocum as he saddled his horse and got the bounty hunter's pony ready to hit the trail again. Squinting at the stars, he saw it was about an hour past midnight. With luck, he could reach somewhere with a telegraph by daybreak.

Slocum wasn't too sure what this place was. Tularosa was miles off to the south. The Valley of Fires stretched black, rocky, and ominous to the west. Carrizozo might be an hour or two away, but this small nameless town had a telegraph station.

"I can get it through to El Paso for you. Fifty cents," the man said, peering at the flimsy yellow sheet over the top of his glasses. "If you want, you can add another few words. Same price."

"That'll do," Slocum said, hating the idea that the telegraph operator had to read the message to Lizbeth in order to send it.

"You part of the posse?" the telegrapher asked, sitting himself behind the banks of lead-acid batteries that filled the small office with nose-twitching odor.

"Not exactly. My interests are more . . . monetary," Slocum said.

"Oh, a bounty hunter," the telegrapher said, satisfied.

"You see many through here? Bounty hunters?"

"Big Mike swept through here like a summer thunderstorm a week or so back. You know him?"

"Big Mike O'Leary?" Slocum snorted. How well he knew the bounty hunter. "I've made his acquaintance. We didn't hit it off too good."

"I can understand that. He's an ornery cuss." The man's fingers flew against the "bug," sending the dots and dashes along the wires to El Paso. "There. You want to wait for a reply? We ain't got a hotel here, but you can sleep over at Old Man Kendall's stable for a dime a night."

"Sounds like heaven to me," Slocum allowed. He chewed his lower lip, considering if he ought to wait for any reply from Lizbeth. She might not even be in El Paso, choosing to wait in Mesilla. He felt the noose tightening on his throat at the thought of staying too long in any place where the law might happen by.

"Well? You waitin' for a reply or not?"

"Reckon so. If it doesn't come by sunup tomorrow, I'll move on." Slocum had been careful wording the telegram, talking only of "your brother" and "stormy times ahead" when referring to Billy Quince and John Wesley Hardin. He hoped Lizbeth would understand his caution.

He walked up and down the length of the town's main street in five minutes. If there were fifty people here, it would surprise him. He found a decent enough place to eat, though he could have eaten boot leather and thought it good after living on nothing but skinny rabbits and slow lizards for the last few days. The last tin can of beans had been

devoured soon after he had cut down Big Mike. Slocum
had thought he needed the strength to make it across the
mountains and toward a place where he could send a telegram.

Slocum stepped out onto the hot, dusty street after finishing his meal in time to see the telegrapher waving to
him, a yellow sheet in his hand.

"Come on over, mister. Got a reply for you!"

Slocum hurried. The man thrust the telegram into his
hands. Slocum read it quickly and went cold inside.

"Bad news?"

"You might say that," Slocum answered. The way he
read the message told him John Wesley Hardin was riding
into El Paso, coming from somewhere in south Texas. That
much he had guessed. Otherwise Quince would have lit out
from the territory fast to go find the notorious gunman. But
the rest of the message was what filled Slocum with dread.

Lizbeth intended to ask John Wesley Hardin not to kill
her brother. She might as well ask the sun not to rise or
the moon to set. Worse, by bringing Billy Quince to the
gunfighter's attention and warning him of Quince's inten-
tions, it guaranteed another killing for Hardin. Hardin
didn't have eyes in the back of his head, but there were
men who believed he did.

"You got a reply to this one?" asked the telegrapher.

"No, no reply," Slocum said, knowing where he had to
ride. And the telegrapher had read the destination in his
expression too.

Slocum mounted and headed south, not bothering to hide
his trail to El Paso. The telegraph operator was no man's
fool. That warned Slocum that he had to do what he could
to keep the law off his neck if he rode back into El Paso.

Two miles outside the small town, Slocum spotted the
telegraph lines running south. A single message to the El
Paso marshal would bring out a reception committee for
Slocum he would as soon avoid. He dismounted and cut
off a two-foot hunk of rawhide from a longer piece dan-

gling from the bounty hunter's saddlebags. He eyed the telegraph pole, took a deep breath, and started shinnying up it like a monkey.

Reaching the wire, Slocum took his time tying the hunk of rawhide around the insulated copper strand. Then he cut the wire. It took another few minutes to bend the severed wire around the rawhide so the rest of the wire dipped only a little more than usual. He eyed his work, then slid down the pole to study it from the ground.

He could not tell where he had spliced in the rawhide and cut the wire. Good. Anyone riding out to repair the line would have a devil of a time spotting the break, giving Slocum that much more time. And no message about the curious stranger and his suspicious telegrams would be sent to the marshal in El Paso.

It didn't give him much of an edge, but it was better than nothing.

Slocum mounted and rode south again, this time through the malpais in order to avoid Tularosa and prying eyes there. He wanted to reach El Paso without shooting it out with Marshal Hanssen's or any other posse on his trail.

12

It was hot, and Slocum was suffering. The bounty hunter's horse had died of lack of water, and his own wasn't in good condition. Even riding at night and resting during the blazing hot day wasn't working. The Jornado del Muerto was well named—and Slocum was miles and mountains away from it. The desert was a killer, no matter what it was called, no matter which side of the mountain range it lay on.

He tossed and turned as the heat worked on him. He turned over, froze, and saw he shared his bedroll with a scorpion. Carefully reaching out, he drew his six-shooter and used the butt to crush the poisonous monster. Even in death, the curved tail still managed to swing around and sting at gunmetal. Slocum wiped off the ichor and flopped flat on his back, staring through the branches of a mesquite above him, promising shade and lying by small measures here and there. The only other greenery in sight was some spindly creosote bushes. Even the stunted oak trees had failed to leaf out this year, owing to the heat and drought.

Slocum came upright, and his horse reared as the gunshot echoed down the arroyo where they camped, seeking any shade they could. He wiped at the butt of his six-gun again, just to be sure, then thrust it into his cross-draw holster.

"Not a posse," he told his skittish horse. "Not one after us, at any rate." Marshal Hanssen would have been certain to have every rifle aimed at him before giving the word to fire. Slocum would have been boxed in with nowhere to run. But he saw and heard only the sluggish movement of dried vegetation in the hot wind—and then another gunshot in the distance.

He ought to avoid any possible collision with the law or another bounty hunter, but he was getting mighty dry and his horse needed water too. As hard as it was to imagine, there were others out in this burning sun. Settlers moving from a hell they knew to another they didn't, thinking they were going to paradise. Men like Slocum, simply drifting in search of the next sunset and a horizon they had never seen. Even trade rumbling north, coming up from Hueco Tanks and the Butterfield Stagecoach terminus.

If this was a wagon train being attacked, Slocum knew he was closer to El Paso than he had thought. Or he might have stumbled across Billy Quince by accident. He rode slowly, unable to push his horse toward the now-rapid gunfire faster than a walk.

In less than a mile he saw the freight wagon pulled up, its team rearing and pawing and causing all kinds of devilment. Neither driver nor shotgun guard were to be seen, but from under the heavy canvas covering the bed poked two gun barrels. One was a derringer and useless, but the other looked to Slocum like a .44, a six-shooter capable of causing a man a world of woe should the heavy slug rip through his body.

He looked around, trying to figure out the problem. He saw a man wearing a bandanna over his face crouching some distance away from the wagon, a rifle in his grip. The man fired twice more, then leaned the rifle against a rock and drew his six-gun.

"All I want's your money! Don't make this any harder than it had to be!" the road agent yelled.

"You ain't killin' us!" shouted back a man under the

tarpaulin. "You cut down the driver and the guard! We ain't lettin' you murder us too!"

"I didn't kill 'em!" the outlaw protested. "They upped and run off!"

"Liar!" The man inside the wagon showed himself, thrust out the heavy .44, and blazed away, not even coming close to the road agent's hiding place. Slocum watched, bemused. It was an inept robbery, but the defense of the life and property of those in the wagon was even worse. The only thing that amazed him was that neither side in the fight had shot himself by accident.

The outlaw jumped to his feet and fired three times. One slug ripped through the thick wooden side on the side of the wagon. This caused a bevy of outraged shouts from those under the tarp. An older woman poked her head out and brandished the derringer. Slocum worried about her because she was as likely to shoot her traveling companions as she was the feckless highwayman.

"Get ready," Slocum said, patting his horse's neck. "This might be more dangerous for us than for them." He drew his rifle, levered in a round, and let out a rebel yell. The horse did the best it could to bring him into the fray at a gallop. No one seemed to notice the gait was hardly more than a trot, but it was good enough to get everyone's attention.

"Get down, take cover, and I'll drive him off!" Slocum shouted to the passengers in the freight wagon. He fired accurately at the outlaw. Seeing real opposition, the road agent let out a yelp and dove for cover. Before Slocum overran the man's hiding spot, the outlaw was gone, leaving behind his rifle.

Slocum scooped it up and walked his horse back to the wagon. The .44 and the derringer were both poking out, aimed at him.

"It's all over. I drove him off," Slocum said. "He even left behind his rifle. Here." He tossed it to the ground beside the wagon. "You folks all right?"

He waited. When there was no answer, he touched the brim of his hat and said, "Glad to hear it. Enjoy the rest of your trip. I don't think the road agent'll be back to annoy you." He wheeled about and started off. The hairs on the back of his neck rose in anticipation of a bullet blowing his head off. Slocum doubted anyone in the wagon recognized him, but they were so antsy, a finger on a trigger might twitch and send him to the promised land.

"Wait, mister! Come on back! We want to thank you!"

Slocum glanced over his shoulder and saw a smallish man with a huge walrus mustache waving the .44 around. Behind him came the woman and her derringer. Following them was a boy hardly ten years old.

"Yeah, mister, don't ride away!" the boy shouted. The woman shushed him. Slocum began to get a clearer picture of what was going on. A family on the way somewhere north, maybe to Santa Fe. From where? He doubted they were from El Paso by the way they were dressed. Somewhere else in Texas was his guess. Maybe Dallas.

He rode back and dismounted to give his horse a rest.

"You don't look the worse for wear and tear," Slocum said. "But then he wasn't much of a robber."

"What are you saying?" exclaimed the woman. "Why, that was none other than Billy Quince!"

"Yeah, mister," chimed in the boy. "He's killed a dozen men, maybe more. Maybe a hundred!"

"Quince?" Slocum took off his hat and wiped sweat from his face. Whoever had tried to rob this freighter, it wasn't Quince. Slocum hadn't recognized the voice—and Quince would have simply ridden up and filled the people with round after round until everyone was dead. He would not have pleaded with them to give up their valuables. He might have taken what they had, but only off their corpses.

"Surely was. They warned us about him. That's why I bought this weapon," the man said, awkwardly swinging the .44 around. Slocum made a wry face at such clumsiness, and hoped the man wouldn't trigger off another round in some random direction.

"My husband doesn't have much experience with firearms, sir," the woman said.

"I'd never have guessed," Slocum said, trying not to sound too sarcastic, for the sake of the boy and whatever faith he had in his father to defend the family honor. "I didn't do much more than shoo the robber on his way. You'd pretty well run him off with your spirited defense."

The man puffed up and stuffed the six-gun into the waistband of his trousers. He winced a little as the hot metal touched his flesh, but tried not to show it for his son's sake.

"Where are the driver and guard?" Slocum asked. "The robber—"

"Billy Quince," the boy cut in.

". . . the road agent didn't shoot them, did he?" Slocum clambered up to the driver's box and failed to find even a drop of blood. The long-barreled shotgun was wedged down in the foot well and took a little work to free. If someone had jumped from the box, his feet might have caused the shotgun to jam in like that.

"They were sure it was that vile Quince," the woman said firmly. "That is why they abandoned us the way they did."

Slocum shook his head in disbelief. Just the name of Billy Quince spooked otherwise courageous men. He settled in the box and worked to quiet the horses. The heat worked on them as much as his gentling, and they soon stood passively, waiting to be on their way.

"You folks pass through a way station?" he called down.

"Not two miles back down the road," the man said. The woman argued with him how far it was. Slocum motioned for the boy to climb up. The boy grinned and hurried up to drop beside Slocum.

"I think your folks need a driver," Slocum said. "They need a shotgun guard too. You up to the task?"

"Sure, you bet!"

"Then get your folks into the wagon. We're going back to the way station."

"But we're heading up to Santa Fe," the boy said. "Pa's got a job as clerk with the territorial governor. Lew Wallace is his name. He's writin' a book about some fella in Rome and—"

Slocum ignored the boy's chatter. He'd had no truck with the governor, and wished he'd had none with the federal marshal in Santa Fe. If he had a jot of sense he'd simply ride on and leave these greenhorns to fend for themselves, but he couldn't do that. He didn't think it would do much harm taking them to a way station. Driving them back to El Paso would be suicidal, though.

He made sure his horse was secured to the rear of the wagon, then got the rig turned and heading back down the twin-rutted road he hadn't even realized existed until he had heard the gunfire. For this he had the would-be outlaw to thank. He might have missed the way station and the water it promised entirely if he had kept on moving at night.

The station came into view. Slocum licked his lips, worrying that a wanted poster or word of an escaped killer other than Billy Quince might have reached them. His mouth was as dry as the desert sand around him, but he didn't have much choice but to keep on. If he abandoned the family now, they would wonder why and ask questions he didn't care to have answered.

"Hello!" Slocum called, waving his hat long before he drove up to the abode hut that passed for a stage depot. His hail got the stationmaster out, rifle ready. "We had some trouble down the trail."

"Who're you?"

"He helped us!" the man inside the wagon yelled as he thrust his head out from under the heavy canvas flap. "He rescued us from Billy Quince!"

"What? Quince! Son of a bitch!" The man motioned

Slocum to drive the wagon around to the side.

The stationmaster approached cautiously, in spite of the family's gushing about how Slocum had saved them from certain death.

"Where're Buddy and Len?" he asked.

"The driver and guard?" Slocum looked to the family to furnish the answer. Their testimony would carry more weight than anything he had to say since the armed man was still edgy and on his guard.

"They left us to the mercy of that terrible outlaw," the woman said angrily, stamping her foot. "If this gentleman had not ridden by and saved us, we would have been slaughtered!"

The stationmaster eyed Slocum suspiciously. "How'd you just happen by?"

"I was resting in an arroyo, waiting for the sun to go down. On my way from up north, heading for El Paso," Slocum said. "Seems the whole countryside is in an uproar over this Billy Quince. Who is he?"

"You ain't heard?" asked the stationmaster. Then he realized this was not likely if Slocum was telling the truth. "No reason you would, if you've been out on the trail. Let's get them horses taken care of and then get on inside for some nice, cool water and I'll tell you a tale that'll curl your toes. Yes, sir!"

Slocum listened, and ate the stationmaster's food and drank his water, and answered questions by asking others and avoided arousing suspicion. Why should a man on the run from a necktie party in El Paso be heading that way? Why would any outlaw running with the likes of Billy Quince help a poor family traveling to Santa Fe? Slocum had everything in his favor.

He listened and he commiserated and he even agreed that it was a miracle they had all escaped Billy Quince's wrath back on the trail. At sundown Slocum was on his way south again, heading toward Lizbeth and El Paso and more trouble than he cared to think about.

•   •   •

It took three more days before he reached the outskirts of the sleepy, dusty border town. Slocum hardly believed it carried such a threat for him as he rode down the main street, hat pulled low and avoiding eye contact with the few fools wandering about in the late afternoon heat. He had decided to enter El Paso now rather than when it cooled off. The chance of anyone noticing anything but the heat now was far less than after they got liquored up and were intent on hunting down someone to pick a fight with.

In spite of his plan, Slocum saw the street ahead was filled with a small throng of people. They were crowded near the door of the First National Bank. Slocum saw several lawmen, including the El Paso marshal, pushing the crowd back. As the onlookers gave way, bodies on the ground became evident.

Slocum stopped counting when he got to four. Unless he missed his guess, he had gotten back to El Paso just a little after Quince.

"Did you see it?" asked a woman from the shade of a boardwalk. "Did you, mister?"

It took Slocum a few seconds to realize she was talking to him.

"No, ma'am, I didn't. Just rode in. What happened?"

"It was him. *Him,* I say." There was no mistaking whom she meant. Even if she had spoken of the devil himself, her tone wouldn't have been any different. "He strutted on in just like he was cock of the walk, he did. I saw it all from over here. He whipped out two six-guns and opened fire without even telling them it was a robbery. It was like he wanted to see them die and didn't care a whit for the money. But he took a bag or two just the same."

Slocum knew then it was no longer a toss-up between the devil and Billy Quince. The devil had more compassion and would have warned his victims before gunning them down.

"Not the kind of town I want to stay in," Slocum said,

wondering how hard it would be to find Lizbeth. He doubted Miss Peabody had allowed her to stay. And it wouldn't have been prudent for the lovely dark-haired woman to return there. The best place for Lizbeth would be across the border with Consuela.

"We got Rangers coming in from Van Horn," the woman told him. "They'll put a stop to this reign of terror since those good-for-nothing lawmen we got cannot." She sniffed and looked as if she had bitten into a persimmon.

Slocum pulled the brim of his hat down a little lower on his forehead and nodded in her direction, heading back in the direction he had come from to avoid the crowd and the deputies in it. Something made him stop and turn back to look.

"Lizbeth!" Her name slipped from his lips before he realized. The woman stood across the street, dabbing at tears running down her cheeks. Even from this distance he could see that her hands shook and she was distraught over this new atrocity.

Slocum also saw that the marshal and his deputies were clearing out the crowd. He wouldn't have much time. The woman who had told him about the bank robbery might not have recognized him, but there wasn't a single lawman who wouldn't pounce on him like a buzzard on fresh carrion if he spotted him. Slocum dismounted and used the horse to shield him from the lawmen's direct gaze.

"Lizbeth!" he called again. She looked up, eyes red from crying.

"John," she said, swallowing hard. "You came back. I . . . I worried that you were—"

He put his finger to his lips and gestured toward an alley. He made his way past one deputy without being seen, and then headed down the alley. In a few minutes Lizbeth joined him. She cried openly again. She threw her arms around him and clung to him, as if she were drowning and he was her only hope of salvation.

"What are you doing here?" he asked. "You ought to

be hiding. The marshal must think you helped break me out of jail.''

"I . . . I heard a rumor that Billy was drinking in a saloon down the street. I c-came to see.'' Lizbeth bit her lower lip. Her hands still shook. "John, it was awful!''

"What? What did you see? It was Billy who robbed the bank, wasn't it?''

"Y-yes, it was Billy,'' she said. Lizbeth clung to him again until the shaking passed and her strength, both physical and moral, returned. A deep breath, and she went on. "I was across the street when I saw him enter the bank. I started to call out to him, but he began killing everyone inside before I could.''

"A good thing. People might have thought you were in cahoots with him.''

"John, he gunned them all down without even a warning. He just killed them, then took the money.''

"And?'' Slocum asked, knowing something more bothered her.

"He came out, eyes wild. He looked around for someone else to kill. All I could hear was the way his six-gun cocked and the thunderous noise when it fired—and the spurs, those damnable spurs. They clanked louder than the six-gun's report, John. I swear it.''

He held her again, but Lizbeth pushed away, hurrying on with her story as if she had to get it all out before she weakened again.

"He was so crazy with the killing he never recognized me, John. He stared right at me and didn't know me. I wasn't anything more than another target for him. H-he raised his six-shooter and aimed it right at me. He saw me and didn't know me.''

"What happened?'' Slocum asked, sensing there was something more bothering Lizbeth.

"He pulled the trigger,'' she said. Slocum went cold inside. "He would have killed me, but he had run through all his ammunition. Billy fired twice more at me before he realized he had used his ammo on the others. He laughed, John, and it was ugly, evil, awful. And he never knew it was me.''

Slocum went cold inside. Billy Quince would have killed his own sister and never known. If Slocum hadn't known before, he did now. The only way this killing spree was going to end was with Billy Quince's death.

13

"You should cross the border and stay with Consuela," Slocum said, looking around the dilapidated house with some disdain. "This is no fit place for—"

"For a woman whose brother is murdering anything that moves?" Lizbeth said angrily. "Maybe this is all I deserve."

"Men might get the wrong idea," Slocum said. Across the street stretched long rows of cribs with the whores and their drunken cowboys and soldiers from the fort. This thick-walled adobe had burned out and been abandoned. Slocum didn't know for sure, but from the look of it nobody other than Lizbeth had been inside for years. It was easier to build a new house than to hoist a new roof and renovate the walls of this one.

"I can take care of myself," Lizbeth said. All her anger drained now, leaving her tired. "I wanted to warn him about facing down John Wesley Hardin. That's what everyone says is going to happen. Billy is going up against Hardin."

"It might be the best thing that could happen," Slocum said slowly. "One of them's bound to die. Either way, it'd be an improvement."

"I know," she said, startling him with such a candid

127

answer. "I don't want Billy to die, but when I saw him he never recognized me. He would have cut me down like I was . . . nothing." She swallowed hard. "I knew then he was lost beyond redemption."

"Then you can go back East and—"

"No!" The sharpness of her answer and the flush that came to her pale cheeks told Slocum her resolve had not faded. "The spurs, John. You promised Consuela and me you would destroy them. Billy might be a lost soul because of them, but I don't want anyone else seduced by their terrible lure."

"The spurs aren't doing this," Slocum said. "I'm not superstitious, but I know what it means to some folks. During the war I knew a sergeant who never went into battle without his good-luck charm on a chain around his neck."

"What happened to him?" she asked.

Slocum stared at her a moment before answering. "A minié ball struck the charm smack on."

"It saved his life?"

"No," Slocum said coldly. "There was only a silver smear left where the charm had been. The ball cut clean through his body and killed him instantly."

"What are you trying to tell me? That there's no such thing as good luck? Well, John, you might be right about that, but I think there is something more at work here. That's no good-luck charm making Billy kill like he is doing. It is pure evil. You heard Consuela. That *brujo* cursed the spurs, and the curse is making Billy this way."

Slocum knew arguing anymore wasn't going to change the woman's mind. She refused to believe that the evil Billy showed so blatantly was present in every man. Some kept it in check. Others denied it totally. Others, such as Billy Quince, gave in to their darker impulses until that weakness of character blighted their life and that of everyone they crossed path with.

Like Lizbeth Quince.

She couldn't admit her brother had gone bad, and Slocum understood.

"I'll go after him. He can't have gotten too far." Slocum snorted in disgust. "I'm sure he's leaving a wide swath of death and destruction behind him for me to follow." What gnawed at Slocum was the stationmaster to the north saying the Rangers were after Billy now. A federal marshal from Santa Fe might give up and go home. The local marshal wasn't likely to risk his neck when he could be breaking up bar fights and serving processes to make a few extra dollars. But the Texas Rangers were as implacable as Billy Quince when it came to their job.

They wouldn't stop until Quince was dead and buried.

Slocum licked his lips, realizing he was being dealt into that hand. He'd been branded as a bad hombre who rode with Quince. He had a death sentence waiting to be carried out, if he got caught. Slocum needed Quince to confess to all his crimes if he ever hoped to get out from under his conviction and death sentence.

That was as likely to happen as the spurs were the cause of Quince's madness.

"I'll be all right, John. I'll wait for you here." She saw his skepticism. "Really. I have this." She drew a small four-shot pistol that looked to be about a .24-caliber.

"Looks like something you could hurt yourself with," Slocum observed, wondering where she had gotten it.

"I'll do what I have to, John. You find Billy and get those spurs away from him. Please." She clung to him again, then gently pushed him away.

Slocum left, wondering if Quince would stick around El Paso waiting for John Wesley Hardin to show up, or if his former partner would be loco enough to go hunting for the notorious gunman. There was no telling what went on in Quince's head now. Slocum would have to ride fast and hope he found Billy before the federal marshal—or the Rangers.

•   •   •

Twenty miles south of El Paso Slocum found Billy Quince's trail. Twenty-one miles south of El Paso he found another set of tracks that looked suspiciously like a posse riding after Quince. Slocum cursed his bad luck. If he had started sooner, if he had been better at sorting out the tracks running parallel to the Rio Grande, he might have gotten to Quince before the law.

"Might not be a posse," he said to himself, but in his gut he knew it was. There were too many bounty hunters and lawmen scouring the country for Quince. No man raised this much of a ruckus without it becoming personal. Slocum had no idea how many widows and widowers and orphans all wanted Quince's scalp. Any lawman stopping this one-man killing spree would rank up there with the Earps in the public imagination—and admiration.

Slocum jumped to the ground and followed the trail more slowly now, not wanting to run across the lawmen's camp by accident. He was glad he had taken this precaution. Less than a hundred yards along the trail he caught the heady scent of fresh-brewed coffee. His mouth watered, but common sense kept him from advancing.

Tethering his horse down by the river, he made his way up the dry banks and worked along on his belly until he saw a dozen men squatting in the shade of cottonwood trees. Two campfires blazed. One held the coffee that had alerted him. Over the other roasted a rabbit. The man turning the spit caught Slocum's eye. Something about the set to his chin, the way he moved, the arrogance in his bearing told him this wasn't one of Marshal Hanssen's deputies.

As the man turned and a ray of sunlight glanced off the badge on the man's vest, Slocum knew the Rangers had arrived.

Slocum wondered what the Rangers intended to do. A second man, equally overbearing, strutted up and flopped alongside the first. The two men didn't speak, but seemed to tolerate each other's company well enough.

Slocum looked back to the fire where the coffee boiled.

He recognized two of Hanssen's deputies. Then he saw the federal marshal making his way up from the river, toting a canteen of water for himself. The lawman glanced in the direction of the two Rangers, seemed inclined to talk to them, then decided against it. He sank down with his back to a tree and drank his water. His deputies left him alone.

Watching the way the lawmen moved told Slocum all he needed to know. Hanssen had found Quince's trail, only to have the pair of Rangers join up. They would hog any reward or notoriety connected with Quince's capture or killing, and Hanssen was not pleased. But the Marshal was from New Mexico Territory and had nothing to say about it. This was the Rangers' territory, not his.

Slocum edged away, then stood and hurried to his horse. He rode across the feeble flow of the Rio Grande and into Mexico, then rode as hard as he could to get south of the posse and then cut back to the U.S. side of the river. The marshal was headed in this direction for a reason. Slocum knew he risked his horse dying under him in the heat, but he had to reach Quince first.

"The damned spurs," Slocum groused, but he was beginning to wonder if Lizbeth and Consuela might not be right. He had ridden with Billy for months and never seen a hint of such cruelty. Then Slocum shook himself like a wet dog. The only power the curse of a *brujo* held was over those superstitious enough to believe. Slocum wasn't the kind to trust in spells or curses.

The Colt Navy riding at his hip was solid and reassuring, and he knew what it could do. That was where his faith rested.

But although his faith might reside in the ebony-handled six-shooter, Slocum began to wonder if Lady Luck had deserted him entirely. Try as he might, he couldn't find Quince's trail. He knew it had to be somewhere in this arid land, but where? The rolling hills and long stretches of emptiness afforded him a good view. He suspected Quince might be heading toward Fort Davis, thinking to find John

Wesley Hardin there on his way up from San Antonio.

But Slocum soon found himself working to cover his own tracks when he realized that Marshal Hanssen's posse was now on *his* trail.

Slocum considered whether Hanssen realized whose heels he now dogged, then realized it hardly mattered if the marshal thought he was on Quince's trail if eventually he found Slocum. Letting the lawmen catch sight of his quarry was enough to get the lot of them stumbling over each other for a good shot at a convicted fugitive from the noose.

Slocum doubled back, used a creosote bush dragging behind to cover his horse's hoofprints in the dry ground, then headed back to the Rio Grande, thinking he could follow the thin trickle of water to throw off his pursuers.

It was nearing sundown, when he ought to be making as good a time as he could along the trail after Billy Quince. Instead, he went to ground, hiding in a grove of cottonwoods, waiting to see if he had to make a run across the river for Mexico to elude the marshal. For over an hour he waited and never caught sight of the posse. This presented Slocum with a new problem. Was Hanssen waiting for him to show himself, or had the marshal given up? Slocum had been good hiding his trail, but was it that good a job?

He waited another hour, knowing the impatient deputies would force Hanssen's hand if they were out there. Slocum climbed into the saddle and returned to tracking Quince, wary of the posse after the murderous outlaw. If it hadn't been for his promise to Lizbeth, Slocum would never have gone after the man.

A half-moon rose and gave Slocum the edge in finding the trail. Quince made no attempt to hide his trail—if it was Quince he followed. Slocum knew this might be a trap laid by the lawmen. He rode along cautiously until he scented a mesquite fire pouring out smoke from upwind. This was the kind of stupid thing Billy Quince would do. Slocum knew it might be another traveler, but he doubted it. The trail led back to El Paso and the rider had been galloping, as if eager to get to some unknown destination.

Instinct told Slocum he had found Quince.

He left his horse behind and advanced on foot, knowing any mistake now would mean his death as surely as if Hanssen caught him. The difference was in time. Quince would gun him down. Hanssen would return him to El Paso to swing from the gallows.

"Damned spurs," Slocum grumbled. He wondered, if he got them off Quince, if he ought to bring them to Lizbeth to show he really had taken them from her brother. She had told him to destroy them. Slocum wasn't a liar, but the temptation to just tell the woman he had done so was great.

He heaved a sigh. That lie would come back to bite him as long as Billy Quince remained on his killing spree. Newspapers would report the mounting number of deaths, and people would spread rumors until Quince was six feet under. He had to get the spurs, and to do that he'd have to kill Quince.

Slocum eased his Colt Navy in its holster, then approached the camp so he could look down into the shallow depression in the sandy hills. Sitting at the fire eating a greasy chunk of cooked meat, Billy Quince seemed not to have a care in the world.

It would be an easy shot. Slocum could draw, aim, and kill Quince without the killer ever knowing what happened. But he had been Slocum's partner and deserved more than to be slaughtered the way he had slaughtered so many others. Slocum drew his six-shooter and rose out of the darkness, ready to confront Quince. If the man insisted on going for either of the six-guns tucked into his belt, so be it. Slocum would have given him a chance to surrender—and to surrender the spurs.

Somehow, Slocum began to wonder if taking the spurs might not return Quince to his old self. But if it did, how could any man live with the knowledge of the killing rampage he had engaged in for so many weeks? Any decent man would rather be dead.

Getting his feet under him, Slocum made sure he stayed in the shadows before starting down the slope toward the fire. He had taken only a step when a deep-throated challenge boomed out.

"Don't move, you ornery cuss!" came one Ranger's order.

"We got the drop on you!" boomed the other Ranger. Both men stepped into the circle of light cast by Quince's campfire. The outlaw looked up, unconcerned.

"Drop the meat and grab some sky. I want to see you—"

"Now, gents, you're rilin' me real bad," Quince said, licking his fingers clean of grease. "You don't mess with a dog when he's eatin'. You could afford me the same courtesy."

"You're worse than a mad dog," snarled one Ranger. Both men advanced, their six-shooters aimed at Quince. Slocum watched in amazement as the lawmen advanced, ready to tie up their captive. That was what they expected. It wasn't what happened.

Slocum had seen gunmen in fights all over the West. Never had he seen a man handle two guns so fast or so expertly. Billy Quince went for the two six-guns thrust into his belt. He dragged out one with his right hand, leaving behind a blur and flash that blinded Slocum.

The Ranger on the receiving end of the bullet stiffened slightly. His eyes widened in surprise; then he sank to the ground as if all the bones in his body had turned to mush.

With his left hand, Quince swung the other pistol around and fired three times, fanning the hammer with the side of his right hand still clutching the other pistol. The first two slugs blew off the second Ranger's kneecaps. As the man pitched forward like a felled tree, unable to run or even take a step, the third slug ripped through the top of his

Stetson and into his brain. He was dead before he hit the ground.

Slocum recognized his chance. He could shoot and get Quince in the back as the gunman stared at the two dead Rangers. But his shaking hand couldn't grip the butt of his six-shooter tightly enough for accurate shooting, and his finger turned sweaty and slipped from the trigger. Slocum's heart pounded like a drum, and he knew fear at facing down another man in a fight for the first time in more years than he cared to remember.

Those Rangers had been killers in their own right. They'd had the drop on Quince, yet Billy had drawn and fired before the Rangers could even pull back on their triggers. His hands had moved so fast they had been blurs.

Billy Quince thrust his pair of six-guns back into his belt, squatted again by his fire to finish his dinner, and ate with animal-like relish as if nothing had interrupted his repast.

Shaken by what he had seen, Slocum stepped back and faded into the dark, not sure what the hell to do.

14

Slocum crouched in the shadows and watched. Billy Quince made no move to check the bodies of the two Rangers he had just cut down with his quick six-shooters. He finished his food, unconcerned about anything in the world. If it had been any other man, Quince ought to have gotten spooked and gone looking for other lawmen. Instead, he seemed not to have a care in the world.

He wiped his fingers on his shirt and lay back, staring up at the stars for a few minutes, muttering to himself. Then he sat up so suddenly Slocum reached for his own Colt. If Quince had discovered him spying, Slocum would have been dead, just like the Rangers. The man moved faster than any human Slocum had ever seen.

But Quince had not detected his old partner in the shadows. He reached down and spun the rowels on his spurs, laughing as he did so. Slocum watched, and found himself hypnotized by the silvery light reflecting off them. The spinning rowels seemed to disconnect from the spurs and whirl away from Billy's heels, taking on a life of their own. Like small silver stars, they hung in the air above the campfire. Slocum blinked, and the mirage vanished.

The rowels were where they should be, clanking on the stems of the spurs behind Billy's boots. Slocum's heart raced at the idea that those spurs did carry some curse from a Yaqui *brujo*. Then he forced the notion from his mind. They were handsome spurs, but they had nothing to do with Quince's quickness nor his kill-crazed ways.

Slocum hunkered down and watched as Billy polished those spurs, never taking them off his boots. The man worked diligently with a dirty rag. When he finished with one spur, he cast the rag aside and stood, going to a fallen Ranger. Billy ripped off the lawman's bloody shirt and tore it into strips. He used these bloody rags to finish the job of polishing his spurs. Only then did he sink back to his bedroll.

Slocum waited, thinking Billy would fall asleep and give him a chance to sneak up on him. He wasn't sure what he would do when he got close enough. Steal the spurs without waking the man? Impossible. Shoot him? Slocum wasn't sure he could do that, considering Billy's blinding speed with his two six-guns. Hogtie him?

Slocum began gnawing on that idea like a dog with a bone. He was good with a rope. He could lasso Billy and drag him back toward El Paso and let Lizbeth take the spurs herself. Even as this thought crossed his mind, Slocum knew that was a cowardly thing to do. He had to get the spurs. He had promised. Honor dictated he do what Lizbeth and Consuela had asked of him—and what he had agreed to.

Rolling away, Slocum slid over the rise and down the far side, returning to his horse. He was shaky from not having eaten. Or so he told himself. Not getting enough sleep and being constantly alert for the sound of hooves on his trail also had worn him to a frazzle. Slocum made a thousand excuses for the way he felt, although deep down inside he knew the real reason.

He was afraid of Billy Quince.

He had been scared before and come through it. During the war he couldn't count the times he had been frightened and had fought on against overwhelming odds. A time or two he had triumphed. Usually he had fought and escaped with his life. Slocum knew this might be a battle like that. He might not win, but he wasn't going to turn tail and run.

As he reached his horse, a plan began forming in his head. It was desperate and unlikely and would probably get him killed, but he was going to try it. If only Marshal Hanssen and his posse would cooperate by taking a few more days to get on Billy's trail.

If only . . .

Slocum slept poorly, coming awake every few minutes throughout the night, but he dared not let Quince get on the trail ahead of him. An hour before sunrise, Slocum stretched cramped muscles, noticed the grumbling of his belly, and pulled a plug of jerky from his saddlebags. The tough, salty meat made him thirsty, but he had let his canteen go empty. He needed to return to the Rio Grande and replenish his water. He had not thought about it before because of the way he'd dodged the Rangers and Hanssen's posse.

Now even the thought of scummy water drew him.

"Later," he said to himself. "Soon." If he succeeded in trapping Quince, he could take all the time he wanted getting water. Crossing into Mexico was the obvious way of avoiding the federal marshal, even if Hanssen came across after them. The Mexicans guarded their territorial sovereignty jealously. With a little luck, Slocum could get back to El Paso with Quince on the other side of the Rio Grande.

When—if—he captured the outlaw. If he didn't, he wasn't likely to need any more water. Ever.

Quince was following the road angling southeast past the Finlay Mountains and the towering peak of Sierra Blanca, heading toward Fort Davis. He seemed inclined to travel the easiest, fastest route, no matter that the law was after him. Still, with his speed and utter ruthlessness, two Rangers had not slowed him. Why should an entire posse?

Slocum counted on Quince's single-minded hunt for

John Wesley Hardin to aid him. He rode along, studying the road to Van Horn. In the far dusty distance rose the Davis Mountains, more a product of his imagination than actual peaks, Slocum suspected. But what wasn't a heat mirage was a small oasis along the road. A clump of trees and a pond of water and the ideal spot for what Slocum intended.

He trotted ahead, then let his horse drink his fill. Slocum washed his face and settled his nerves, then staked his horse out near a patch of blue grama. Taking his lariat, Slocum climbed a tree and sat on a thick limb, looking down at the rutted path leading to the water ten feet below. He settled down for what might be a long wait.

He nodded off now and then, still sleepy from his restless night. But the sound of hoofbeats brought him upright. He drew out his rope and peered down at the trail, waiting as patiently as a cougar on the tree limb for its prey to water.

A curious calm settled on Slocum now that the time to take Billy Quince had come. He knew he wouldn't get a second chance, but that didn't bother him as much as worrying over the damned spurs. It was nothing but superstition that the spurs were cursed, but still he worried.

Then Quince rode under him and Slocum dropped his lasso and tumbled backward off the far side of the sturdy limb. The rope dug into Quince's arms, pinning them to his side. The way Slocum fell while hanging onto the rope jerked the killer out of his saddle and pulled him kicking hard into the air.

Slocum landed on the ground and hastily secured the free end around the tree trunk. Only then did he dare to approach the dangling outlaw.

"Slocum!"

"None other, Billy. You got any good reason I shouldn't just plug you here and now?" Slocum recoiled slightly when he saw how Quince went for his two six-shooters in spite of the rope around his arms and his entire weight holding him securely. Blood seemed to explode from the man's trapped arms as he struggled. All Slocum could think of was a wolf with its leg caught in a steel-jawed trap—chewing off its own limb so it could escape.

Slocum reached up and plucked first one and then the other six-gun from the man's belt. He cast them aside, then danced away to keep Quince from savaging him with the silver spurs. Quince swung around and around, cursing and kicking, lashing out at Slocum as if he were some bucking bronco.

"Settle down. You're only hurting yourself," Slocum said. To his surprise, a calm settled over Billy Quince like some soft, warm familiar blanket.

"You're right, John. I shouldn't fight you. We're partners, aren't we? Go on, let me down. It'll be all right."

Slocum might have bought it except that Quince's eyes retained their hardness. A cunning unlike anything Slocum had ever seen warned Slocum not to lower his guard.

Slocum didn't answer. He fetched Billy's horse and led it back, along with his own. When Quince saw Slocum wasn't going to release him, he began frothing at the mouth like a mad dog and kicking wildly again, the silver spurs flashing like knives in the bright sunlight. Slocum stepped back, figuring Quince would tire himself out soon enough. Again he was astounded by the man's vitality.

Quince didn't so much tire out as give up, hanging with the rope around his arms. The wild look never faded from his face. Blood ran in rivers down his arms, soaking clothing and rope. And the spurs. Those damned spurs.

When Quince subsided for a moment, Slocum grabbed the man's ankles and tried to peel off the dusty boots, gleaming spurs along with them. Quince's frenzy forced Slocum to stop. If he hadn't, either a spur or the toe of a boot would have smashed his face into a bloody mess.

"I can break your legs and get the spurs that way," Slocum told his former partner, malice in his voice. Quince snarled and snapped like a trapped wild animal, hearing nothing Slocum said. "Or if you ride along with me all peaceful-like, I'll let you keep the spurs on. What'll it be, Billy?''

Again the amazing and sudden change came over him. The man turned downright peaceful, dangling like a sack of potatoes rather than struggling like a goosed weasel.

''Whatever you say, John.''

After seeing how mercurial his moods were, Slocum wasn't gulled into believing Quince. He secured Quince's feet under his horse's belly before lowering fully him to the saddle. Slocum worked fast before Quince got circulation back into his arms. Fastening his wrists securely behind his back wasn't likely to be good enough. Slocum tied his arms and then put a rope around Quince's neck, draping the free end around his own saddlehorn.

''You try escaping and I'll drag you by your miserable neck all the way back to El Paso.''

''John, let me go. All I want to do is meet Hardin. I can take him. I'm good enough. He's an old man now. He's slow and fat and tired. He deserves to die!''

Slocum didn't say a word as he mounted his horse, tugged on the rope around Quince's neck, and got the man's horse headed across the river into Mexico. If luck finally came his way, Slocum reckoned he could have Quince—and the spurs—back in El Paso in less than a week. He'd let Lizbeth deal with her brother and decide for herself what to do with the spurs.

For Slocum's part, all he wanted to do was see how nice the summer could be in the Dakotas.

15

"Surely looks nicer down here in Mexico," Billy Quince said sarcastically. Slocum didn't bother replying. He had ridden in stony silence all day, no matter how much Quince chattered on. Putting up with the man's constant profane observations took a toll on him, as much as Slocum tried to ignore him. Quince had nothing good to say about Mexico or Mexicans, and took every chance to belittle both the country and its inhabitants. "You know why it looks nicer, John? There's none of them little brown—"

"Shut up," Slocum snapped, jerking hard on the rope around Quince's neck to emphasize his intent to ride in peace. He was rewarded with a choking sound. Then the small triumph he felt passed when Quince loosened the rope a little and laughed. The killer had intended to goad him and had succeeded.

"You got a mighty thin skin, John. Never thought it of you. You don't have any stomach for what has to be done. Bet you couldn't kill one of them Mexican whores, no matter how hard you tried. Not even if she gave you the clap. Not even—"

Slocum reined back and glared at his captive. "One more word from you and I'll put you on foot. It's a long walk back to El Paso."

"Why you going back there, John? They want you bad.
I heard tell you missed getting your neck stretched by a
couple hours, and the law still wants to hang you, maybe
worse than they did before. How'd you get out of that jail?
It looked like a cracker box to me, but a man as stupid as
you'd have trouble doing it on your own."

Slocum tugged on the rope again, wondering what Lizbeth might say if he returned with the sad news that her
brother had died somewhere on the trip back. For two
cents and a bucket of spit, Slocum would plug Billy Quince
and leave his body on the desert sands for the buzzards.
Slocum sneered as he considered doing this. He doubted
the buzzards would have anything to do with the vile meat
on Billy Quince's bones. Devouring him might gag the flying carrion-eaters.

"Bet you had help," Quince went on when he got his
voice back. He twisted his head side to side to loosen the
rope a bit more. It left a wicked red weal Quince ignored.
His venom drove out any hint of pain. "It couldn't be my
dear sister who sprung you, now could it? Is she sweet on
you, John? She never had a speck of sense. Imagine her
sniffing around after you like—"

Slocum jerked hard on the rope again.

"This is the last time I'm going to tell you to keep that
tater trap of yours shut," Slocum said. "I don't want to
hear anything you have to say."

"Not even that we've had a band of *rurales* on our trail
for the past hour?"

Slocum fixed his cold green eyes on Quince, trying to
determine if the man only taunted him or if it was true.
Mexican troopers patrolled the border and jealously
guarded it against foreign invaders. If they found Slocum
and Quince, they were as likely to kill both of them as let
them go, unless Slocum had enough money to bribe them.
He had only a few crumpled greenbacks in his shirt
pocket—not enough to buy off any greedy volunteer army
officer hunting for an easy way to feather his own nest.

Unable to tell if Quince lied, Slocum heaved the free end of the rope up and over a tree limb. Silently, he fastened the end to the trunk. If Quince's horse spooked, the man would hang. Somehow, Slocum didn't see this as much of a loss, and Quince's horse would have a lighter load to carry.

He heard Quince's choking sounds as the man strained to keep from strangling. Much of it was Quince's way of goading Slocum into making a mistake, and only a little came from actual constriction of the rough hemp around his neck.

Slocum went hunting, drifting through the scrubby brush of the Chihuahua Desert until he climbed to the top of a rise giving a decent view of the trail he had just traversed. Slocum let out a deep sigh. Quince had been uncannily accurate. Three miles back of them rode a small knot of ill-dressed Mexican soldiers. The men had to furnish their own uniforms and having so little money, few wore more than the official shirt or hat scavenged during battles from their fallen *amigos*. But from what Slocum could see of the ragtag soldiers, all carried rifles and had bandoliers filled with ammunition crisscrossing their chests.

He wasn't in trouble with the law in Mexico. The commanding officer might let him ride on, but probably not without a big bribe or a lot of convincing that Billy Quince was a prisoner on his way back to El Paso. Slocum turned grim at having to make that revelation. A prisoner meant reward, something a poor soldier might just kill to win.

For the first time since capturing the murderer, Slocum realized what a spot he was in. He was a convicted killer trying to lead a cold-blooded assassin back into Texas while avoiding a federal marshal.

Since Quince had killed two Texas Rangers, there would be a full company of those implacable lawmen on their trail. Marshal Hanssen might hesitate to enter Mexico in hot pursuit, but the Rangers wouldn't if it meant avenging the deaths of two of their own.

Slocum knew what he had to do if he wanted to stay alive. Kill Quince, take the spurs, and ride hellbent for leather with them to El Paso and Lizbeth. He dared not be slowed by Quince—or even found with the man. Slocum's hope of getting the killer to confess and lift the death sentence riding on his head seemed nothing more than a foolish dream at the moment.

He ought to do that. Slocum wheeled about and trotted back to the tree where Quince still made gurgling noises. When the killer saw it had no effect on Slocum, he stopped, twisted around in the saddle, and sneered.

"I was right, wasn't I? The greasers will—"

Slocum kicked Quince's horse in the rump. The horse jumped, threatening Quince with being pulled apart like a chicken. The rope tightened around his neck, and his feet were still bound under his horse's belly.

"I told you to keep that dirty mouth of yours shut." Slocum retrieved the end of the rope and tied it again to his saddlehorn. "We're heading back across the border. Hanssen and the Rangers will be farther south hunting for you. We can sneak back into El Paso and—"

"Yeah, Slocum, that's your style, isn't it? Sneaking like a lily-livered coward!"

Slocum edged his horse closer and pulled Quince's bandanna from around his throat. It had partially protected the flesh there. No longer. Slocum stuffed it into Quince's mouth and knotted it firmly behind the man's head.

"I warned you." With that Slocum trotted off, tugging on the rope. Quince had no choice but to let his horse follow. Slocum headed north, then angled back to the northeast, thinking to reach the Rio Grande and the dubious safety of the U.S. side. He wasn't sure he believed Hanssen was that far to the south of where they would reenter the country. The federal marshal had shown himself to be a diligent tracker, and might have figured out Slocum's plan and doubled back. If he had, Slocum would ride straight into the lawman's open arms.

A whoop and a holler from behind warned Slocum that the *rurales* had spotted them. He urged his horse to greater speed, but the animal was tired and had been abused constantly. The horse stumbled, but tried gamely to respond. All Slocum got out of Quince were muffled grunts and what sounded like curses about the Mexicans. Where that hatred had come from, Slocum didn't understand. When he had ridden with Billy Quince the man hadn't had a fanatic bone in his body. No longer. He took special glee killing Mexicans and Indians.

"Alto!" cried the *rurale* officer. The words and a hail of bullets came about the same time. The soldiers weren't good marksmen and the range was great, but they kept firing. Even a blind man could hit a target if he shot enough times.

"The river's a mile off. We can make it," Slocum shouted over his shoulder to Quince. He couldn't tell if his former partner found any comfort in that. Quince bounced along, forced to stay on horseback using only his legs. He bobbed and bounced around, looking more like a child's rag doll than a human being.

Slocum cut back and forth to avoid the sustained rifle fire, then abandoned that tactic in favor of a direct run to the river. He dared not let the Mexican soldiers overtake him, but less than halfway to the Rio Grande's sandy, dry bed Slocum saw he wasn't going to make it. The horses of the *rurales* were rested, and narrowed the distance steadily. His own began faltering, its gait shot to hell by sheer exhaustion.

He slowed and heard the thunder of hooves behind. Not wanting to do it but seeing no other choice, Slocum reined to a halt, drew his rifle, and prepared to fight off the soldiers.

"You are under arrest!" cried the officer, galloping hard now with his men following closely. Slocum was a good shot, but he could never hope to get all the *soldados*. He would have to content himself with dropping the officer and hoping the others were discouraged after seeing their leader killed.

Slocum raised the rifle and aimed the best he could from horseback. His dun-colored horse began crow-hopping, making accurate fire all but impossible.

"Go on, Slocum. Kill the little brown bastards!" Quince had forced the bandanna from his mouth. His lips curled in pure hate. Slocum drew back, not sure what to do.

Then it was decided for him. Bullets sang through the air. For a moment, Slocum was confused. The slugs came from behind him, tearing through the attacking squad of *rurales*. Their officer motioned to his men, and they broke off the attack. The officer shouted something Slocum did not understand, then followed his men back into the hills.

Slocum lowered his rifle, wondering what was going on.

The cold voice told him real fast.

"I can knock you outta the saddle if you so much as twitch a muscle, Slocum," came Marshal Hanssen's promise of death.

Slocum lifted his hands, rifle away from his shoulder. His horse nervously pawed the ground and slowly turned. Behind them, crossing the river in violation of national integrity, Hanssen had led his posse to the rescue. If it could be called a rescue at all. Slocum was again the marshal's prisoner.

"Glad to see you got some sense left," Hanssen said: His men quickly circled their two prisoners, six-shooters leveled. Slocum knew the mere hint of flight would get him killed. But he still considered it. Better to take a bullet, even in the back, than to die with a noose around his neck.

"I was taking him to El Paso," Slocum said.

"By avoiding the law on the American side," Hanssen said. "You're not playin' me for a fool, Slocum. We seen you and came after you." Hanssen spoke harshly, but frowned as he studied the way Slocum had trussed up Billy Quince.

"You two have a fallin' out?" Hanssen finally asked.

"With that coward?" snarled Quince. "He ain't got guts enough to ride with a man of my ability."

Slocum wanted to explain, but held his tongue. Quince might just do what Slocum had hoped—and without using torture.

"You two aren't ridin' as partners anymore?" asked Hanssen.

"I wouldn't be seen dead with a coward like him. We split weeks back."

Slocum held his breath, hoping Quince did not mention the stagecoach robbery that had gone sour. Slocum had not had any part in murdering the passengers, but the law wouldn't see it that way.

"You been doin' all the shootin' and killin' on your own?" Hanssen asked.

The marshal almost had to step back as pure vitriol poured from Billy Quince as he confessed to every killing in loving, hate-filled detail. Slocum's eyes widened when he realized Quince was like a collector. He not only remembered every murder, he cherished them and compared one against another, and plotted how to do the next even better.

"So Slocum had nothing to do with—" began the marshal.

"Slocum's not fit to ride with even a Mexican," Quince said, hurling his vilest epithet. "I don't know what all he's done since we split up, but it was only my own damned bad luck he caught me."

"Everything he's said is the truth, Marshal," Slocum said.

"Looks like you might be an innocent bystander in this circus, Slocum," Hanssen said slowly. "If a man like you could ever be called innocent."

Slocum wasn't going to argue with either the marshal or Quince. Let them think what they wanted as long as he got out of the murder charges against him in El Paso.

"You mean Slocum ain't gonna swing, Marshal?" asked a deputy.

"That'll be up to the judge to decide, but I got to tell him what all Quince's been sayin'. The sidewinder is a one-man disaster."

"I'm just too much of a man. Let me go, Marshal, and I'll take care of your biggest headache. I want John Wesley Hardin. I can take him."

"So our information was right. You *were* ridin' south to tangle with Hardin." The marshal looked utterly perplexed any man could do such a dumb thing. "Quince, you gotta learn to never squat down whilst you're wearin' your spurs. Throwing down on Hardin is a one-way ticket to the boneyard."

"For Hardin it will be," retorted Quince. "I'll gun him down just like I did the others." He launched into a description of his crimes all over again. Slocum saw more than one deputy in the posse glance away, either in disgust or upset over his constant confessions. More than one of the men had lost a wife or child or brother to Quince's outlaw six-shooters, Slocum figured.

"Let's get on back across the Rio Grande," Hanssen said uneasily. The marshal, like many of his men, showed how flustered he was at Quince's loud, proud, bloody confession.

They rode in silence, save for Quince's constant verbal barrage. As soon they struggled through the sandy bank on the U.S. side, the marshal motioned to a pair of his men to gag Quince again.

"I see why you rode with him like that. He's a foul-mouthed hombre."

"We going to El Paso?" Slocum asked.

"Where else? Qunice's got a date with the hangman, just like you did. It's danged lucky we found you and he gushed out like he did, Slocum. Otherwise, I might have spent a goodly portion of my life huntin' for you."

Slocum nodded. He glanced back and saw the sun reflecting off Quince's spurs—the spurs he needed to destroy.

"It'd be something good to remember him by if you'd let me pass those spurs of Quince's along to his sister." At this Quince thrashed about and forced the gag from his mouth.

Hanssen glanced at the spurs and seemed to shudder. Then he faced forward and urged his horse to a faster gait.

"You can have 'em after we swing the son of a bitch. Not right takin' a man's spurs 'fore he's dead."

"Thanks, Marshal," Quince said. "I want to die with my boots on and the spurs are a part of me. Wouldn't be fitting if you upped and killed me without lettin' me wear what I wanted to the gallows."

Slocum saw Quince was laughing at him for the attempt to get the spurs away. Settling in and riding along in silence, Slocum considered ways of getting the spurs before Quince was hanged. He wanted to get out of this dry, dusty death-filled land as fast as he could. If he satisfied Lizbeth over the spurs, that would let him drift on now that Marshal Hanssen had agreed to clear him.

Four days later they rode into El Paso, saddle weary and ready for a rest. The way the crowds formed around them told Slocum what a celebrity Billy Quince had become. They ignored Slocum pretty much, even after the town marshal tried to throw him in the same cell with Quince, intending to hang the pair of them together.

"You got it wrong, Marshal," Hanssen said. "Fetch the judge and we'll talk this over. Slocum here's not innocent as a lamb, no, sir, but he was bringin' Quince in when we found him."

The El Paso marshal squinted at Slocum. "You mean this owlhoot was turnin' in his own partner?"

"Former partner," Slocum said. "He's done me wrong too. I didn't kill the people I was accused of."

"Quince confessed to it. Bragged even. He's *proud* of all the killin', and he can give details nobody'd know 'cept the real killer." Hanssen shivered in spite of the heat inside the small jailhouse. "He downright enjoys tellin' the details. Never seen a killer like him before."

The judge arrived. Slocum kept his own counsel until Hanssen had convinced both the El Paso marshal and the judge.

"Here's a paper saying you're free to go. I'd recommend you leaving El Paso and never coming back," Judge Magoffin said, signing the pardon with a flourish and passing it over to Slocum.

"I want to claim Quince's spurs for his sister. Something good to remember him by," Slocum said, knowing Lizbeth would insist he destroy those well-crafted spurs. Slocum thought the notion of a curse was crazy, but melting the spurs in a smithy's forge was a way of proclaiming all ties with Billy Quince were gone. It might be good for Lizbeth.

The judge spat accurately into the cuspidor at the corner of the marshal's desk, then rubbed his chin.

"Can't see anything wrong with that. When you gonna swing the bastard?" the judge asked.

"Soon, I trust," Hanssen said. "It's been a powerful long time since I seen my family. I want to get back to Santa Fe."

"Sunrise tomorrow," Judge Magoffin said decisively. "Why do we need a trial when we know we got the son of a bitch? He's confessed." The judge used the butt of his six-gun as a gavel to rap on the desk. "There. Now let's go wet our whistles. I can't remember a summer this hot or dry since—"

He was cut off by gunshots from the cell block.

"What in tarnation is that?" the judge asked. He turned as the door swung open. Billy Quince stood in the doorway, a six-shooter in each hand. He opened fire, wounding the judge. Another slug lodged in Marshal Hanssen's belly, doubling him over. The El Paso marshal died trying to fumble out his own six-gun.

In spite of the shock at seeing Quince free, Slocum was faster than any of the lawmen. He dragged out his Colt

Navy and got off two fast shots. Both missed. Rather than trade rounds with Quince, Slocum stumbled out into the street, yelling for help. A dozen deputies came running.

"Quince's loose. He killed the deputy guarding him. And Marshal Hanssen and your marshal," he gasped out.

One deputy eyed Slocum suspiciously, still not trusting him in spite of what Marshal Hanssen had said, and then all hell cut loose when Quince burst out into the street. He carried a double-barreled shotgun, and fired repeatedly until the barrel turned cherry-red and he cast it aside. By then the lawmen outside the jailhouse had dived for cover. Slocum waited to get a good shot at his former partner, but Quince was too wily. The chance for a clean kill never came.

But Quince's chance to escape did. Billy Quince stole two horses and shooed off the rest of the posse's mounts, then rode down the street shooting wildly at anyone or anything that moved.

All Slocum could see as Quince galloped from town were bright silver sparks kicking off the rowels of those damned spurs.

16

"The marshal's dead," called a deputy poking his head into the jailhouse. "But that federal one's still alive. So's Judge Magoffin. He only got a slight wound in his side."

Slocum stood stiffly, aware of several six-guns aimed at his spine. He had come out of the jail a few seconds before Quince. He didn't begrudge the lawmen the notion he had a part in helping Quince get away, but that didn't make him any less uneasy.

A muzzle crammed into Slocum's side. "Let's go see what all's happenin' in there," ordered a deputy with a grim set to his mouth. For two cents he would pull the trigger and worry about Slocum's role in the escape later.

A small crowd already circled the fallen Marshal Hanssen. The federal marshal looked up and pointed at Slocum.

"He . . . he saved my life. He kept Quince from shootin' me and the judge. Take that hogleg out of his back, Clay, and give 'im a medal or something." Hanssen sank back to the floor, blood staining the wood floor. A doctor pushed his way through the crowd. He reeked of cheap booze, but worked with a sure hand.

"What's it going to be, Doc?" Slocum asked. "Is he going to make it?"

"I'm a damn fine doctor, yes, sir," the man said, his

155

bloodshot eyes staring up at Slocum. "Of course he's gonna make it. It'll take more 'n a bullet or two to slow this mangy cayuse down. He's gonna be good as gold in a day or two, thanks to my expert doctoring. Who's payin' this time?"

"The judge is shot too," a local deputy said. "Looks like you're gonna have to bill the mayor."

"I jist left him at the Cross-Eyed Jacks down the street. Better go see to gettin' my due 'fore the mayor drinks it up." The doctor stood and pointed at Hanssen. "Git him and Judge Magoffin on over to my surgery. The marshal needs some rest 'fore he hits the trail again. All the judge needs is a bit of plaster on that scratch."

"Scratch!" growled the judge. "I'm bleeding here. This is no scratch. I'm sorely wounded!"

"Like I said, the mayor's gonna pay dearly this time," the doctor said, chuckling as he rubbed his hands together. "Now git 'em over to my office."

The deputies from Santa Fe took the marshal away. The few local lawmen all tended to their dead boss and the irate judge: No one seemed to notice the lack of concern over hunting down the killer responsible for the carnage.

Slocum went to a cabinet and rummaged through it, finding ammunition for his Colt and for the Winchester sheathed on his saddle. He waited to see if anyone mentioned his minor theft. When no one did, he stepped back into the hot El Paso sun and stared down the street in the direction taken by the fleeing Billy Quince. Slocum knew he could follow the trail of death and destruction the man left, but on two horses Quince might be able to make it to Tombstone before he slowed.

But Slocum didn't think so.

Quince had headed south before to cut off John Wesley Hardin so the two could have a showdown. Hardin had the reputation Quince wanted for his own. Billy Quince wasn't going to stray far, not until he had it out with the notorious gunfighter.

Slocum mounted and rode slowly in the other direction. He thought he knew where Quince would show up next. All he had to do was find Lizbeth Quince.

It took the better part of the day before Slocum located the dark-haired woman. She had stayed in the burned-out building for a few days before moving on. He tracked her to a small, shabby hotel at the edge of town. It was hardly better than the abandoned adobe, but at least she didn't have to fight the scorpions for a place in the bed.

"John!" she cried, seeing him from across the small hotel lobby. She rose and took a step toward him. Then her hand shot to her mouth and Lizbeth wobbled a little. "You didn't find him, did you?"

"I found him," Slocum said. He took her arm and steered her back to a chair. For the next twenty minutes he told Lizbeth all that had happened to him and how her brother had escaped—again.

"He's a slippery cuss," Slocum said. "Being so willing to shoot down anyone facing him makes it hard hanging onto him."

"At least the law isn't after you anymore," she said. Her bright eyes fixed him. After licking her lips, she asked the question he had been dreading. "The spurs, John. Did you get the spurs?"

"No," was all he could say. Lizbeth slumped as if he had punched her. She straightened, and he saw resolve firming in her again.

"I can't ask you to continue this hunt, John," she said. "I'm letting you out of your promise to Consuela and me."

"The spurs don't matter to you any longer?" Slocum asked. He read the answer on Lizbeth's lovely, strained face before she found the right words.

"Of course they do. But I'll find my brother and get the spurs from him. I don't know how I'll do it, but I will."

"Find him or get the spurs?" Slocum asked. "Remember how he was the last time your paths crossed."

"I know, John. He didn't even recognize me because he was so intent on killing. But I *will* get those spurs and destroy them. Who knows how many other lives will be ruined by the curse?"

"I don't go back on my word," Slocum said tiredly. "Besides, I know where your brother's most likely to show up next."

"What? Where?" Lizbeth leaned forward and captured his hand in hers. "Tell me. I want to know. I *need* to know!"

"Unless I miss my guess, he's going to come looking for you."

"Why? He didn't know me. He—" Her blue eyes went wide with horror as she realized. Billy Quince had sampled evil of every kind, except killing his own blood. "He wants to kill me, doesn't he?"

Slocum wondered if Quince wasn't looking for something more than just killing his sister, but he said nothing about that. Lizbeth was upset enough at the idea that her only remaining relative was such a debased human being.

"We can make it work to our benefit," Slocum said. "Setting a trap for Billy might work. It did for me once before."

"What should I do? Go out and let everyone know where I am? I hadn't realized you were free of those terrible murder charges so I stayed hidden. The adobe became far too uncomfortable for me, and I moved here." She gestured, indicating the modest hotel. "It's not much, but it is better than being forced to watch all the illicit activity that went on across the street."

"No need to advertise your presence. If you did, Billy might smell a trap. Let him work it out for himself. He might get overconfident if he thinks he's ahead of me— and you."

"When is he likely to be along, John?" she asked, but the tone of her voice had changed. She dropped her gaze demurely, but then looked at him with seething desire.

"It took me hours to track you down, and I knew where to start looking. I doubt Billy could be here until after sundown." Slocum looked at the Regulator clock dolefully ticking across the lobby. The hottest part of the day drove most El Paso citizens indoors out of the sun for a siesta. Slocum doubted he and Lizbeth would do much sleeping if they went down the hallway to her first-floor room.

And they didn't.

The cramped room afforded little space other than for the bed. Slocum wasn't going to complain, though. He found himself pressed up close to Lizbeth. Her eager fingers worked at his gunbelt. It had barely fallen to the floor before she was skinning off his shirt and working on the buttons holding his jeans.

"My turn," he told her when he felt the hot wind from the hotel room window blowing across his naked chest. He stroked across her cheek and caught at the flow of her long, black hair, pulling her head back so her face turned up to his. Slocum kissed her hard.

For a moment, Lizbeth struggled, as if she wanted to run like a frightened animal. Then her desires fueled the kiss, and she returned every ounce of passion Slocum was giving. Their lips crushed, and her tongue peeked out between her lips to tease and torment Slocum's.

From one mouth to the other danced their tongues until they were both panting.

"You're overdressed for such a hot day," Slocum said. He worked at the top button on her blouse. He felt her breasts rising and falling faster as he worked. Slocum bent down and used his teeth on the next few buttons, letting the milky swell of her breasts slowly appear. When they swung free of her blouse, he turned his attention from the cloth to the softy, creamy flesh. He licked from the broad bases all the way to the top, then teased the nubbin there with the tip of his tongue.

"Oh, John, I need you so. No more of this. I want you now. Now!" she pleaded. Her fingers clutched fiercely at him, dragging him to the bed. They landed hard, the springs squeaking under their combined weight.

Slocum stripped off her blouse entirely, then ran his fingers under the waistband of her skirt. She arched upward, letting him pull the unwanted clothing away from her curvy rump. When she sank back to the bed, she was gloriously naked and ready for him.

He stared at her for a moment, then gave in to the urges mounting in his loins. Slipping quickly between her thighs, he reached down to the fleecy triangle there and rubbed gently. She moaned again. Lizbeth's legs lifted so her knees rubbed on either side of his sweating body.

Slocum's hips moved forward with a life of their own. He sank fully into her seething interior, and grunted at the moist heat and tightness of the fit. He held himself up on his arms, staring into her eyes. She smiled and then strained upward to kiss him fervently. They kissed until neither could stand the strain of his hidden manhood.

Slocum retreated slowly, then reasserted himself. The friction of entry burned along the length of his shaft. Lizbeth started moaning in pleasure, and Slocum picked up the pace. She was the most beautiful, beguiling woman he had met in years. Sharing mutual danger cemented the bond between them and added spice to the lovemaking. Either of them might die at any moment because of Billy Quince.

This might be the last time for them, and they savored every thrust and turn and twist, every caress and kiss, until they both exploded with pent-up emotion. Together they strove, two melding into one. Finally spent, they lay side by side, arms around each other. The hot wind gusted over Slocum's back and dried the sweat, cooling him. On the other side Lizbeth pressed close and warm.

"That was wonderful, John," she said in a low voice.

"It was wonderful, but—?" he asked, sensing the unspoken question in her tone.

"When will Billy find us?"

He had no answer to that. Instead, Slocum pulled Lizbeth

closer and simply held her for what might be the last time.

"As much as I want this to go on, John, I just can't tolerate it right now." Lizbeth pushed away from him and sat up on the bed. Slocum ran his fingers up and down her backbone, outlining each of the vertebrae. Her skin felt like silk under his rough fingers. Lizbeth shivered. He wasn't sure if it was his touch or the knowledge that Billy would find them sooner or later.

Probably sooner.

"Why don't you take a bath?" he suggested. "This is good weather for it. You'll cool off afterward."

"I'm not sure I want to be *that* cool, now that I've experienced real fire," she said, reaching back and stroking over his tautly muscled belly. Her fingers drifted lower, then pulled back. "All right. I'll take a bath. I wish you could join me, though."

"Later," Slocum said. "When this is behind us."

Lizbeth dressed and left the tiny room, going to tell the clerk to draw her a bath. Getting hot water on a day like this, although it was nearing sundown, would not be hard. Slocum dressed quickly, and settled his six-shooter in its cross-draw holster. He practiced a few times, whipping out the deadly Colt, cocking and aiming it at the room's door-knob.

He was fast. But Slocum remembered watching Quince throw-down on the two Rangers. They had the drop on him and he still drew, fired, and killed them in a spectacular fashion. For Quince it was little more than stepping on a bug.

Slocum was fast. But not that fast.

He settled back on the bed, legs stretched in front of him. Thinking of Quince didn't help much. He let his mind wander, and this settled his nerves more than anything else could. Dreading Quince's lightning-fast draw would only make him hesitate when he could least afford it.

Slocum checked his pocket watch and frowned. Lizbeth had been gone a spell. He went to the door and opened it a fraction, looking out. It wouldn't do her reputation any good if a man was seen leaving her sleeping quarters. The clerk was nowhere to be seen. The only thing that struck Slocum was the hot air trapped inside the hotel.

He stepped into the hall, started for the lobby, then turned. Something wasn't right. Drawing his six-shooter, Slocum walked along the corridor on cat's feet until he reached the door at the end of the hall with a crudely written sign saying "BATH" hanging on it.

Slocum started to knock to see if Lizbeth was still inside. Caution again held him back. He went to the side door and looked outside. His heart leaped to his throat. Two hard-ridden horses stood out there. Slocum didn't recognize either horse as being stolen during Quince's escape from the city jail, but he jumped to the inevitable conclusion.

Billy Quince was in the hotel. With Lizbeth.

Slocum licked his lips and went to the bath door. Gingerly trying the knob, he found the door unlocked. With his left hand he turned the cut-glass doorknob and shoved the door open hard. His six-gun rested in his right hand, ready to fire without quarter.

He wanted to scream out in frustration. The room was empty. Suds had overflowed the tub and still dampened the floor, but otherwise the room was empty.

Slocum swung around, wondering where Quince and Lizbeth might have gone. His eyes widened when he looked back down the corridor. Reflected in the Regulator clock he saw Lizbeth's head, her hair in wet disarray from her bath.

He didn't know what to do. If he spooked Quince, the man would kill Lizbeth without so much as a fare-thee-well. That might even be why the killer had sought her out. He had experienced every other killing thrill. All that was left was slaughtering his own sister and watching her die.

If Slocum did nothing, Quince might kill Lizbeth. And if Slocum acted, he might spark a gunfight with Lizbeth caught in the middle. It took him only an instant to decide.

Better to act than to do nothing. Six-shooter out and cocked, he strode down the corridor and into the lobby. Slocum swung about, went into a crouch and—did nothing.

"I figured you'd be out sooner or later, Slocum," sneered Quince. He had a gun pressed to Lizbeth's temple and held her from behind. At least she was dressed again. Slocum had no shot that didn't endanger the woman more than her brother. "I see I was right about the two of you actin' like swine in rut. Is she good, Johnny? Is my little sister good at—"

"Let's take this outside, Quince. There's no need to put Lizbeth between us. It's me you want anyway."

"No, Slocum, no, it's not. You're dog shit to me. I want Hardin. I kill him, I'm famous!" An insane edge came to Quince's words.

"I know where Hardin is. You didn't know that he'd already got into town, did you?" Slocum lied. He had to rattle Quince and force him into a mistake. Quince's left arm circled Lizbeth's throat, and he shoved the muzzle of the six-shooter in his right hand smack against her head.

Quince's eagerness to go up against the gunfighter betrayed him. Lizbeth twisted just a little when his grip on her throat lessened. This allowed her to kick out and get a few inches between them.

Slocum took the shot. Quince yelped in pain as Slocum's slug ripped along the length of his right arm. The six-gun fell from Quince's suddenly numbed grip, and he stepped back. Slocum would have fired again, but Lizbeth spun and lashed out at her brother, pummeling him with her tiny fists.

"Get down!" Slocum shouted.

Lizbeth shoved hard against Quince's chest, sending him reeling back through the window in the small sitting room. She fell to her knees as Slocum rushed to her side.

"Get him, John. Get him—and the spurs!"

Slocum thrust his pistol through the window, ready to shoot Quince. The man had turned to smoke on the wind and was nowhere to be seen. But Slocum guessed where

Quince headed. He ran to the desk to tell the clerk to fetch the law, then saw Quince had beaten him to the man. Head almost severed by a savage knife slash, the clerk lay dead in a drying pool of his own blood.

Cursing under his breath, Slocum ran the length of the hotel down the corridor, crashed into the back wall, and bounced out the side door. He whirled around, hunting for Billy Quince. Slocum steadied when he saw the grinning killer peering down the barrel of a rifle.

"Mexican standoff, John," Quince said almost happily. "You have a cocked six-shooter ready to shoot. I have a rifle trained on you. We kill each other and who benefits?"

"What are we going to do, Quince?" asked Slocum. He considered going ahead and shooting Quince. He would hit the man, but would he kill him? Or could Quince squeeze off an accurate shot? Slocum didn't know how to play it.

"This is no fun, John. Killing each other proves nothing."

"Give me the spurs and you can ride on out," Slocum said.

"The spurs? Hell, no, Slocum! I keep them. What's so important about them? You know I like 'em, and it would get my goat if you took 'em? Is that it? You just want to rile me?" Quince whipped up his rage. Slocum saw Quince's finger turning white around the rifle trigger. He got ready to trade lead.

"I want to get out of this alive," Slocum said, not telling Quince anything he didn't already know. "But if it comes down to it, I'm not afraid to die. Are you, Quince? You know I'm a good shot."

"Let's do this right, Slocum. You holster your six-gun, and I'll drop my rifle."

Slocum remembered the way Quince had outdrawn the two Rangers. Fast, Quince was fast. He slowly thrust his Colt Navy into his holster and waited as Quince set his rifle down.

Quince rolled his shoulders and shook out stiff muscles

in his right arm. It bled sluggishly where Slocum had wounded him. From the way Quince flexed his fingers, Slocum doubted the man would be at any disadvantage. And he was fast, faster than lightning.

"You shoulda known better than to cross me, Slocum," Quince said, squaring off. "There's nobody what can beat me to the draw. When I finish you I'll take John Wesley Hardin. I got a question for you to answer first."

"You trying to talk me to death, Billy?"

Quince laughed harshly. "Answer me this, Slocum. Is Hardin really in El Paso?"

"How the hell should I know?"

"That's what I figured," Quince said.

Slocum settled himself and got ready to draw. He heard a small scratching noise behind him and went for his six-shooter, clearing leather and getting a shot off before Quince could even draw.

"Lizbeth," Quince said, eyes going wide as the pain from Slocum's bullet tearing through his chest finally reached his brain. Even distracted by his sister and pain, Quince had managed to whip out his gun in a smooth, fast draw and fire. Quince's bullet had missed Slocum's head by scant inches.

Billy Quince stood stock-still, looking from his horrified sister to his smoking six-shooter to the red flower growing on his shirtfront. A smile twisted his lips as he tried to speak. No words came out. Then the killer collapsed and died.

17

Slocum stood for a moment as if he had frozen into a granite statue. His Colt was the only substantial thing in the world, everything else curiously dim or hazy or feeling a thousand miles away. He tried to sort through what had just happened and found it all a jumble. Quince was blazingly fast, yet Slocum had outdrawn him. Lizbeth pushed past Slocum and went to her brother, kneeling to roll him over and hold his head in her lap. Slocum watched and tried to understand how this murderous son of a bitch could have so loving a sister.

He couldn't. And he couldn't get it square in his head how he had actually outdrawn a man able to kill two Rangers who already had the drop on him. It might have been Lizbeth distracting Quince for a vital instant. Or maybe Quince had wanted Slocum to kill him, though that argument held no water when Slocum thought of all the others Quince had killed as mere practice to get ready for John Wesley Hardin.

"Maybe I was faster," Slocum muttered to himself. It was hard to believe, but it had to be true. Quince lay dead on the ground, not John Slocum.

He thrust his six-shooter back into his holster and walked to stand beside Lizbeth. She sobbed quietly and rocked

Billy's head back and forth. She finally looked up at Slocum, and for a terrible instant he was worried that she would blame him for what her brother had become—and the way he had died. But the dark-haired woman bit her lower lip, sniffed, and finally found the right words.

"You did what had to be done, John. Nothing would have stopped Billy. In a way, I'm glad it was a friend who did it and not some lawman." She sniffed again, and tears ran down her cheeks. "Or a hangman. I couldn't have endured watching my brother die on the gallows. This was better."

Slocum said nothing. Better would have been never starting the killing spree. Better would have been working for a few paltry dollars and grub at the Lazy V all summer long. Best for Billy Quince might have been never being born.

"I'll find an undertaker and arrange for a funeral," she went on. "He doesn't deserve much, but he was my brother and I want to see him put into hallowed ground."

"Might be better not to say too much to the undertaker about who his new client is," Slocum pointed out. "Billy's not got the best of reputations in these parts."

"I understand." Lizbeth laid her brother's head into the dust. The half-smile, half-sneer had become his last facial feature. Even in death he looked evil. Slocum refrained from putting another slug into him, just to be sure.

Lizbeth went to the boots and struggled to unfasten the silver spurs. Her fingers might as well have been oversized sausages for all the dexterity she showed. Slocum gently pulled her away and aimed her toward the hotel.

"Find a horse and get into town. If you get him buried before you tell the law, it'll be easier on everyone." Slocum knew the deputies would swarm over the hotel because of Billy's vicious last killing. The hotel clerk would have to be buried in pieces because of Billy. But if Lizbeth turned her brother's body over to the law, they might take it into their heads to drag the corpse through the streets as a retaliation for the wanton killing Quince had done.

Lizbeth might never be able to bury Billy, and making sure she could struck Slocum as the best thing that could be done for the woman now. Once he was in the grave, she could put him and all he'd done behind her.

"The spurs, John. Get them off and destroy them." She pointed to Quince's boots. The spurs shone brighter than the sun, sending off sparkling pinwheels all around the man's feet.

"I'll get them," he promised. Lizbeth nodded and went on her way. Slocum wasn't certain she could get Billy buried before questions got asked. It might look as though the clerk had shot Billy in self-defense before dying, and then the killer had died later of his wounds. Slocum would never have bought such a tall tale, and he doubted any one in El Paso, all its residents bent on revenge, would either.

Marshal Hanssen might agree to the cock-and-bull explanation just to be finished with Billy Quince, but Slocum doubted that too. No jury would ever convict Slocum of killing Quince, but if he could avoid another trial, that would suit him just fine.

Slocum dropped to his knees and began working at the leather straps over the tops of Quinces boots. The spurs refused to come off. If the Rio Kid had stolen them off a sleeping man, he had been a master thief. As Slocum considered using a knife to cut the straps, he popped the right spur free. He held it up like a trophy so it caught the full sun. The light dazzled him.

Blinking, he lowered the fancy silver spur and got to work on the left one. This came free more easily. Slocum stood with the pair of spurs in his right hand, weighing them, wondering if they had been made of pure silver. They might be worth a hundred dollars or more. But pure silver was soft. Slocum used a fingernail to scratch one.

"Alloy. Sterling silver maybe," he decided. Slocum looked more closely at the intricate silver work, fascinated by the design. He understood why Billy had not wanted to part with these. The Yaqui silversmith had been a master. Slocum spun the rowels, and watched the curious illusion of sparks flying off the sharp tips.

He glanced over his shoulder. Lizbeth had already headed out to find an undertaker. She would protest, but Slocum had to try on the spurs. He had never worn such elaborate, expensive ones before. He knelt and fastened them to his boots.

The boots were scuffed and dirty. But the spurs made them look like new ones fashioned by an expensive San Francisco bootmaker. More than that, wearing them made Slocum feel good. He looked down at Billy Quince's corpse and then spat on him.

"You were such a fool," Slocum said contemptuously. "You thought you were better than me. I outdrew you like you were some greenhorn who'd never handled a six-shooter before."

Slocum laughed, the mirth welling up from deep within him. He laughed at the world and Billy Quince, and even at himself for thinking such a pitiful man could ever have scared him, even for a second. Walking to his horse, he mounted and looked around. He had promised Lizbeth he would get rid of the spurs, and he would. Breaking his promise wasn't in him, but for once he wanted to walk like a man and let others see how successful he had become.

Slocum wanted everyone to see the spurs and know their wearer was the gunman who killed Billy Quince.

He rode proudly into the center of El Paso, hunting for a saloon.

Outside the Purple Cow Dance Hall he paused for a moment, then dismounted and threw back the tall doors so they banged on the inner walls. Slocum got everyone's attention as he stood outlined in the doorway, the sun slanting in from behind him. He turned from side to side showing off the spurs.

"Drinks for everyone," he called. There was a moment of silence, then a loud cheer and a rush for the bar. He walked over, the men parting in front of him.

"What's the celebration, mister?" asked the barkeep, not really caring because he had two dozen thirsty patrons to keep watered. "Must be powerful big."

"I just gunned down Billy Quince," Slocum said.

This brought another blanket of silence over the saloon. From the far end of the bar, someone said, "You're Slocum, ain't ya? The one that was convicted of killing—"

"The judge admitted that was all a mistake. Quince did that killing. And I just killed Quince."

"You tellin' the truth?" asked the barkeep.

Slocum spun, reached across the bar, and caught the man by the throat. He squeezed. Hard.

"You calling me a liar?"

"N-no," gurgled the barkeep. "Seems like we'd heard something about Quince dyin', that's all."

"I'm telling you. We faced off, we drew, and I put a bullet through his putrid heart." Slocum grinned, and knew it was intimidating by the way men backed from him, their free drinks untouched on the bar. "He put me through hell and I paid him back for it. He's not going out killing anymore, thanks to me, John Slocum!"

Slocum looked around. A surge of anger shot through him. He tried to control it, then decided it wasn't worth the effort.

"What's wrong? My whiskey not good enough for you? Drink!" He drew his Colt in one swift movement. The speed startled even Slocum. Hardly had he reached for the ebony handle of his six-shooter before it came into his grip, cocked and ready to kill.

Slocum's hand shook slightly to keep his finger from drawing back on the trigger and putting one or two of these fools out of their misery. They were too stupid to live. He'd be doing society a favor if he put them six feet under.

"Don't go gettin' antsy on us, Mr. Slocum," said the barkeep, rubbing his neck. "Here's my best whiskey. Best in El Paso. All for you." He pushed the bottle across the bar. Slocum grabbed it and downed a swallow. He spat it out.

"You call this good? Pig swill, that's what it is." Again he fought the urge to kill such vermin. How could any decent man pass off such rotgut as real whiskey? The barkeep deserved to die for such a lie.

Slocum's hand shook a mite. He relaxed and shoved his six-shooter back into his holster. It had felt so damned good making the others in the bar dance to his tune. All his life he had been pushed around, made to eat crow, turned into an outlaw by a corrupt carpetbagger judge intent on stealing the family land back in Calhoun County, Georgia. Now the tables were turned.

They'd respect him. They'd respect him or die!

Slocum whirled around. Again his draw was faster than any man's he had ever seen. The six-shooter came into his hand and he fired, blowing out a window in front of two men trying to sneak out.

"You can drink with me or you can die where you stand," Slocum said. Then he laughed. One of the men had fouled himself. "You filled up your boot that quick? You been drinking beer?"

"Y-yes, sir," stammered the man.

"Get back here and drink whiskey. *My* whiskey." The way Slocum said it, it wasn't an invitation, it was an order. The six-shooter in his hand reinforced it. Both men hurried back and gulped down the whiskey.

"G-good," said the one with the wet trousers. "Th-thanks, Mr. Slocum."

"Drink up," Slocum ordered. "Where's the piano player? Get some music playing. I'm celebrating."

He strutted to a table and sat in a straight-backed chair. Hoisting his feet to the table, Slocum watched as the rowels on his spurs spun hypnotically. It amazed him how wearing such fine spurs could change his attitude. He had let others walk all over him before he put them on. Slocum began to appreciate how Billy had felt.

What he needed to go with such fine spurs was a suit of clothes. Maybe like a gambler's, with fancy headlight diamond stickpin and silk cravat and a coat that cost a hundred dollars. Even then the outfit wouldn't match these fine spurs.

"Mr. Slocum," called the barkeep. "The drinks you ordered."

"What of them?"

"You owe twenty dollars. If you want, I can run a tab and you can pay later, but I need to know."

"You ought to *give* me the whiskey. I'm famous, you stupid son of a bitch. Men will flock here to see where the man who killed Billy Quince came to celebrate."

"Quince," grumbled the barkeep. "Who was he? Some filthy little backshooter."

Slocum blasted to his feet, his pistol coming out in a move that pleasured him like something sexual. Like something better than sex.

"You saying it wasn't anything to kill Billy Quince?"

"I—" The barkeep went white under his tan. No words formed on his lips. Then Slocum laughed and thrust his six-gun back into his holster.

"You're right. Even the village idiot can be right at times," Slocum declared, laughing. The others joined in weakly. "Who was Quince anyway? Some cowboy who went crazy, that's all. For it to mean anything, I have to do what Quince couldn't."

"What's that?" asked the barkeep.

"I need to find John Wesley Hardin and see if he's anywhere near as good a gunman as he claims."

"Mr. Slocum, that's not such a good idea," the barkeep said, turning whiter than a bleached linen sheet now. "He's about the best that ever lived. He's better than good."

"I heard he was riding into El Paso. I want him." Slocum fought as a tiny voice in the back of his head cried out about the folly of such a gunfight. But the haughtiness he felt after cutting down Quince grew minute by minute.

Hardin was only a man, and probably not as good a one as Billy Quince.

Slocum had killed Quince. That meant he could kill Hardin too. He felt up to it. His hand was fast, his aim was deadly. Who was John Wesley Hardin anyway?

"Who's looking for me?" came the level, cold question from the doorway. Standing there was a man dressed in a black cutaway coat, the side pulled back to reveal a worn oak handle on an equally well-used six-shooter.

Slocum knew he should say nothing. As if from a distance listening to another man talk, he heard himself say, "It's not you I'm looking for."

"You said you wanted to meet up with Hardin."

"Hardin's a man. You're nothing but a snake crawling in after being out in the sun too long."

"I'd heard there was a man named Quince gunning for me," Hardin said, voice brittle with anger. "You Billy Quince?"

"I just killed him not two hours ago," Slocum said. "If you're really John Wesley Hardin, I reckon I get to kill you too."

"Outside, take it outside!" cried the barkeep, diving behind the bar for cover if shooting started. The others in the Purple Cow Dance Hall went through windows and the back door to get away. Slocum wanted to laugh at their cowardice. Not a one of them was man enough to face a gunfighter like Hardin.

If this was even Hardin. He didn't look as tough as his reputation made him out to be. If anything, he looked like a tinhorn gambler more likely to turn tail and run than to fight.

"That's a good idea. Let's go outside where everyone can watch," Hardin said. He stepped back, turned, and strode away fast. Slocum knew he ought to have drawn and shot Hardin in the back, but that wouldn't show how good a gunman he had become.

Two Rangers? That was the best Quince had done. John

Slocum would show how easy it was to take down a man with more reputation than skill.

He stepped into the hot sun. Hardin was already twenty paces away, facing him. A hot wind kicked up swirls of dust along the street, pulling Hardin's coat away slightly from his angular body. The gunman squinted slightly in the bright sun.

"You can either kiss my ass or you can draw. I don't much care which," Hardin said.

Slocum laughed harshly as he stepped into the street. He was the center of attention. From behind windows hundreds of frightened pissants watched. They were too cowardly to fight a man like Hardin. Slocum wasn't afraid. He was confident. He was the fastest gun who'd ever lived. He would put John Wesley Hardin six feet under as all those yellow-bellied cowards watched.

He squared himself in the middle of the street, concentrating on the gunfighter sixty feet away. A flash of fear— or was it prudence?—tried to insinuate itself. He pushed it away. He was the best, and this would prove it.

He'd polish his spurs with John Wesley Hardin's blood.

"Any time you're ready," he called to the gunman.

A slight twitch of Hardin's hand was all the warning Slocum got. He grabbed for his Colt. Never had he drawn faster. Never had he whirled the muzzle around and brought it to the target faster. His left hand fanned across the hammer, bringing it back and letting it fall to get off the shot. The killing shot. The shot people would remember for years to come.

The shot that killed John Wesley Hardin.

Slocum felt his trusty six-gun buck in his hand, but something was wrong. Dreadfully wrong. The strength in his legs went away fast, and the world spun in a crazy circle as he fell heavily to the street. Distant pain welled up in his chest, and it was hard to breathe, and the bright sunlight began to fade.

18

Pain. Pain was everywhere, but it wasn't as frightening as the darkness. Try as he might, Slocum could see nothing but the thick veil of blackness all around him.

From the distance he heard soft, faint voices, but did not recognize them. Angels? Had he died and gone to Heaven? The notion struck him as funny. That wasn't where he was headed, not with a smoking six-gun in his hand and murderous intent in his heart.

Murderous intent and a bullet, he amended. Vague wisps of memory returned. He had been shot. Hardin had been faster by half. Why had he ever believed it would be any different?

The voices rose in volume, then disappeared. Slocum knew real fear then. Those voices were his only contact with the world of the living. If he heard them, if he understood what they said, he wouldn't be taken away into the sea of utter blackness and the eternal void it promised.

He tried to call out, then sank down, falling into himself.

How much time passed, Slocum did not know. His nose twitched at the scent of whiskey fumes. Eyes fluttering, he focused on the doctor he had seen in the El Paso marshal's office, the man who had rushed off to get his pay from the mayor.

"I do declare, I think you must be part cat. Nine lives and all that. Surely wasn't any skill on my part, but I'll cut your tongue out if you repeat that," the doctor said hastily. "You tell everyone I can bring back the dead and I'll have more business than I can handle." He snorted in disgust and took a pull on a bottle half filled with amber liquid. "What good's working all the time if I can't enjoy myself with a snootful of booze and a lady or two, eh?"

"I'm alive," Slocum said. He spoke forcefully, but the words came out like a frog's croak.

"Looks like. Can't figure why you're so consarned lucky. That bullet went plumb through you. Didn't do a dime's worth of damage, but I'm gonna charge you more 'n that, trust me on that."

"Hardin?"

"Damned fine shot. I was watchin'," the doctor said. "He cleared leather and shot you slick as pig snot. You were quick, no doubt about it, but he was faster. Why'd you do a damnfool thing like go up against Hardin? He's got a reputation, you know."

"I know," Slocum said. "The bullet—?"

"Went straight through. Bounced off a rib along the way and busted it, but you must ride under a lucky star. Didn't puncture a lung or anything important, but I bet you feel like a mule kicked you."

"Yeah."

"You rest up. You rest and I'll have you and the Santa Fe marshal out of here in a day or two."

Slocum tried to ask more. Anger flared in him, only to die down quickly. He tried to remember why he had faced Hardin and ever thought he could outdraw him. Then sleep crept up on him. He fought the encroaching darkness unsuccessfully.

He awoke with a start. Sitting next to him was a vision of loveliness. Lizbeth Quince sat reading a book. She looked up when he moved.

"John, calm down. Don't strain yourself. The doctor says your wound might reopen and that the broken rib . . ."

"Hurts," he managed to say. He took a drink of water from her. It made his throat feel better, but his chest ached and a darkness deep within him blossomed. He had been cheated. He should have killed Hardin.

And he would.

"My clothes," he said. "Get my clothes."

"Soon," Lizbeth said. "The doctor will let you go in a day or so. He says you are mending well."

"I'm going to kill him," he said savagely.

"What?" Lizbeth's eyebrows rose in shock. "You can't mean you want to find Hardin and have it out with him again?"

"That's exactly what I mean," Slocum said. His body betrayed him, but his spirit was more than willing. "I don't know how he did it, but I'm faster. I can take him. And I will. He can't humiliate me like this!"

"You wore the spurs," she said, red lips pulled into a thin slash. "You were supposed to destroy them, and you put them on. They made you go after Hardin."

"No, it wasn't like that," he said, knowing he was lying. "He called me out. He insulted me. I can't let him get by with that!"

"I spoke with those who saw it all, including the bartender. Mr. Samuels is a very nice man, for all his bragging. But his telling is different. The spurs made you go after Hardin. Admit it, John. The curse made you do it."

Anger welled in him, but he controlled it. Unlike before, he felt a small sliver of self-control now.

"How long since I wore the spurs?" he asked.

"Five days. You had a fever for a while," she said.

Slocum hardly believed it. Five days since the gunfight?

"You must reassert your own good sense over the curse, John. Fight it. Billy couldn't, and it killed him. I don't want to lose you too." Tears welled in her eyes.

Irrational anger flooded Slocum. Hardin caused this. He

made Lizbeth cry. There'd be hell to pay when Slocum got on his feet. John Wesley Hardin would be a dead man!

Then Slocum forced away the unreasonable rage. He knew what had happened. Hardin would never have noticed him if he hadn't sought out the gunfighter, as Billy Quince had.

"Where are the spurs?" he asked.

"I have them here," Lizbeth said, holding up a burlap bag as if she had an enraged wolverine in it. "I refuse to touch them, but I feel as if some strange heat comes off them. It makes me uneasy, indignant, even angry. There *is* a curse on them, John."

"I'll destroy the spurs," Slocum promised. "You were right."

Such a lengthy conversation, filled with emotion as it was, tired him out. He sank back to the bed and slept. Deep inside came the slavering, wrathful beast born from the spurs, but this time he forced it away.

This time.

"Seen men heal faster," the doctor said, breathing his whiskey-heavy breath in Slocum's face, "But not often anyone heal up so clean. You got a tiny pink puckered scar right here"—he tapped Slocum's chest—"and a larger one in the back where the lead came out after racin' round your rib cage. Other 'n that, no one will notice." The doctor made a wry face. "With the scars you got already, you'll have to point these out if you want to draw attention to them."

Slocum tried to lift his right arm. Pain jabbed into his chest.

"Don't go raisin' that arm, by the way," the doctor said needlessly. "You'll be able to hold a six-shooter one of the days, but not for a while. Maybe not for a month or longer, until you get some strength back."

Slocum walked around, testing the limits of his recovery. He experienced a little giddiness, but the real hindrance came from the broken rib. If it hadn't cracked as the bullet rolled around it, he would have died. He was lucky. Then he looked to the table across the room where Lizbeth had left the burlap bag with the silver spurs.

He felt as if an evil radiance flowed from them. It took all his willpower to keep from opening the bag. Instead, Slocum dragged it behind him on the floor, then outside, where he left it on the ground until he could get his horse from the livery down the street.

Picking up the bag as if it held mad rattlesnakes, he slung it over his saddlebags, not even bothering to put it inside. Slocum heaved a deep breath. The magnetic draw of the spurs was almost more than he could withstand.

Almost.

He rode from town after stopping at a general store, past Fort Bliss, and into the foothills of the Franklin Mountains. Every foot of the way he wanted to reach back, open the bag, and take out the silver spurs the *brujo* had cursed.

They would slip onto his boots smooth as silk, he knew. And he would be even faster. He would be quick enough on the draw to take that sidewinder John Wesley Hardin.

Slocum kept riding until he reached an abandoned mine. He dismounted and gingerly picked up the burlap bag. Walking to a shaft, Slocum swung the bag around his head a couple times, wincing from the pain. Then he let the burlap bag fly free. The bag with spurs in it clattered a dozen feet into the shaft, then fell down a slope. From the echo the hole might be a hundred feet deep.

It hardly seemed close enough to Hell to suit Slocum.

He took the two sticks of dynamite he had bought in town from his saddlebags and carefully fixed the blasting cap. A foot of black miner's fuse gave him a full minute before detonation. He clumsily lit the fuse using a lucifer, and tossed the explosive down the shaft. He hurried out, waiting in the hot sun. The explosion was satisfying, collapsing the shaft on top of the spurs. But it wasn't enough.

He worked a while tying a rope around the wood support

at the mouth of the mine. He looped the free end of the rope around his saddlehorn, and let his horse tug while he used an iron rod to pry and poke at the support.

When the timber gave way, dust belched from the mouth of the mine. From deep within the earth came a grinding sound that Slocum felt more than heard.

"Good riddance," he muttered, glaring at the closed-in mine. Even then, were dynamite and tons of rock enough?

He mounted and started to ride back down the rocky mountain slope, then halted. He still felt the call of the spurs. It wouldn't take that much to dig out the spurs, he told himself. Just a few days working. Pick and shovel. And then he would be invincible again.

John Wesley Hardin would die. So would anyone else standing in his way.

Slocum twisted fast in the saddle and let the pain from his broken rib wash away the insane urge to retrieve the silver spurs. He rode back to El Paso and Lizbeth, wondering if he could ever ride far enough to be free of the curse.

JAKE LOGAN
TODAY'S HOTTEST ACTION WESTERN!

J. R. ROBERTS
THE GUNSMITH